What people are saying about the *How to Ruin...* books by Simone Elkeles

"Fresh, fun and fabulous! Guaranteed NOT
to ruin your summer vacation!"
—Mari Mancusi, author of *Boys that Bite*

"I highly recommend *How to Ruin a Summer Vacation*.
It reads easily, as if watching a good coming-of-age movie."
—*JVibe* magazine

"A fun read that also digs deeper into complex emotions."
— *Kliatt*

"Amy's thoughtfulness and depth raise this book above
most of the chick-lit genre."
—*VOYA*

"...the choice for teens who seek realistic YA fiction..."
—*School Library Journal*

SIMONE ELKELES

How to Ruin Your
Boyfriend's Reputation

flux
™
Woodbury, Minnesota

First Edition
Fourth Printing, 2011

Book design by Steffani Sawyer
Cover: © iStockphoto.com/Lóránd Gelner
Cover design by Lisa Novak

Flux, an imprint of Llewellyn Publications

Library of Congress Cataloging-in-Publication Data
Elkeles, Simone.
   How to ruin your boyfriend's reputation / Simone Elkeles.—1st ed.
     p. cm.
   Summary: During the summer between her junior and senior year of high school, spoiled Chicagoan Amy Nelson-Barak volunteers for Israeli military boot camp when she learns that her boyfriend, a commando in the Israeli Defense Force, will be at the same military base.
   ISBN 978-0-7387-1879-8
   [1. Military bases—Fiction. 2. Basic training (Military education)—Fiction. 3. Israel—Fiction.] I. Title.
   PZ7.E42578Hm 2009
   [Fic]—dc22

                                              2009023853

Flux
Llewellyn Publications
A Division of Llewellyn Worldwide Ltd.
2143 Wooddale Drive
Woodbury, MN 55125-2989
www.fluxnow.com

Printed in the United States of America

To my mom,
who taught me life is an adventure.
You are definitely a warrior woman!

Acknowledgments

I can't thank Karen Harris and Ruth Kaufman enough for helping me so much with this book. I also want to thank Roni Yeger, who I drilled with relentless questions, and Meko Miller, for brainstorming with me and kicking my butt during my personal training sessions.

There wouldn't be this continuation of the *How to Ruin* series if it weren't for Brian Farrey, Andrew Karre, and Kristin Nelson. Thanks for letting me give Amy and Avi another adventure together!

Other people who have helped me with this book are Marilyn Brant, Pammy Levinson, Erika Danou-Hasan, Omer Schechter, and Moshe Schechter.

Last but not least, I must thank all of the Israeli soldiers who put their lives on the line for their country. I truly wish you and your neighbors a future filled with peace.

---

*A vacation without parents is like a chocolate
brownie without the nuts—absolutely perfect!*

Hi, my name is Amy Nelson-Barak. My mom is a Nelson
and my dad is a Barak and just in case you were wondering, I'm aware I have two last names. If you don't know
me, I'm a seventeen-year-old American teenager with red,
white, and blue blood running through my veins. You're
probably wondering why right now I'm on a bus in Israel
on my way to an Israeli military boot camp.

Yes, I did say I'm in Israel. No need to rub your eyes
and reread that.

And yes, I did say boot camp.

And before you think it's a boot camp for teens with
behavioral disorders, I volunteered for this summer program all on my own. (Although my parents often accuse

me of being a total drama queen, I don't think that counts as a true behavior disorder.) My friends signed up, too. Normally I wouldn't go anywhere near a program with the word "military" in it, especially during the summer between my junior and senior years of high school, but when I realized what military base the boot camp is held at, I jumped to sign up—as a volunteer trainee.

You see, my boyfriend Avi is Israeli. He's in the IDF— Israeli Defense Force—and since I live in the good ol' US of A (Chicago, to be exact), I haven't seen him since he visited me over five months ago. He's a commando, he's nineteen years old, and is just about the hottest, most gorgeous gift God has ever put on this planet. And he's all mine. Well, to be technical, the Israeli military owns his body until he turns twenty-one, but I own his heart. And he owns mine.

So I got this letter from Avi a few months back. He told me that after parachute training he's going to be at Base Nesher. He said if I was visiting Israel this summer, unfortunately he didn't think he could get any time off.

Then, when my best friend Jessica, along with this girl Miranda and my best guy friend Nathan (who I kissed once…okay, three times…but we're just friends), told me they were signing up for a program in Israel that included ten days in basic training boot camp, I laughed at them. I mean, what kind of idiot would go to a military boot camp on purpose?

But guess what? It's at Base Nesher—the same base Avi is at! When I figured that out, I begged my father to sign me up. I haven't told Avi that I'm coming—it's a surprise. I can't wait to see his reaction when he sees me. He's going to be as excited as I am!

I'm so thankful this bus is air conditioned and we have big, cushioned seats for the three-hour ride. We're on the bus with forty other American teens (half are girls, half are guys). The trip is called *Sababa*, which translates to "cool, awesome, a great way of life" or something like that. The tour starts out with the boot camp, then the rest of the summer is spent exploring and touring the country.

The director of the *Sababa* program gave me special permission to sign up for the boot camp portion of the trip only, because after boot camp I'll be staying at my aunt and uncle's house on their *moshav* (kinda like a community farm) in the Golan Heights. So I'll be with family while Miranda, Nathan, and Jessica spend the rest of the summer on the *Sababa* tour.

"Amy, I think Miranda is gonna puke," Nathan tells me. He's sitting next to Miranda, who has had anxiety about the boot camp part of the vacation. She's been stressing about it since we took the plane from Chicago to Tel Aviv (with a ridiculously long layover in New York). Miranda's a tad bit, uh, I don't know how to say this in a politically correct way… let's just say she's in the upper sixtieth percentile on the weight chart hanging in the nurse's office at our high school. (Probably closer to the seventy-fifth, but who's counting.) She's afraid they're going to ration her food at boot camp and make her run until her extra, overflowing muffin-top disappears.

I lean over my best friend Jessica, who's blocking my view of Miranda. "Miranda, it's not going to be like Camp Meltaway. I promise."

Miranda's parents sent her to a fat farm between seventh and eighth grade and she's never gotten over it. The girl cannot survive on granola for snack food. Believe it or not, during her second week at Camp Meltaway, meek and timid Miranda got caught trying to hitchhike into town in search of fast food.

Miranda smiles a little at the sight of a candy bar I pulled from my backpack. Seriously, one day I'll teach her that moderation is "the key" to weight loss. She can have a candy bar every day…just not three of them in one sitting.

Now for me, personally, if I could only get "the key" to smaller boobs (without surgery, since I'm not a fan of getting my little pinky parts cut off and reattached, thank you very much), I'd be the first in line. Yes siree, we all have our little personal issues, things we'd like to change or need to change about ourselves.

"I brought extra Kit Kats," I say, holding up the candy bar. Okay, so the label says *Kif-Kaf* in Hebrew, but it's the same thing.

Jessica slaps my hand down. "Don't show her that."

"Why not?"

"Because she wants to lose weight, Amy. Don't sabotage her."

I roll my eyes. Sometimes my best friend has to be enlightened. "Jess, you heard Nathan. Miranda is so scared she's about to *puke*. I'm just trying to comfort her."

"So comfort her with words and friendship, not candy bars," Jess whispers. "That stuff is poison."

Is she kidding me? Chocolate is my favorite comfort food. Well, it's actually #2 because everybody knows sushi is at the top of my list. Not all sushi, just spicy tuna rolls with little pieces of tempura crunch inside. Nothing, not even chocolate, beats that.

I rummage through my backpack. "Have you seen *these*?" I say, creating suspense as I slowly pull out a *Kif-Kaf* bar wrapped in a white package instead of the usual red one. "It's a Kit Kat bar in *white* chocolate, Jess. They were almost sold out at the store, but I found this one lonely package mixed in with the regular ones. I know you love white chocolate as much as I do." I wave it in front of her nose. "Smell the white chocolate... crave the white chocolate."

"I can't smell anything. It's still in the wrapper."

"I'm saving it for a special occasion."

Before I can stick my rare white chocolate find back in the special zippered compartment in my backpack, Nathan reaches across the bus aisle and snatches the *Kif-Kaf* out of my hand. "Cool, white chocolate Kit Kat. I've always wanted to try one of those. Thanks!"

"Give that back!" I yell.

Nathan, who is a total and complete dufus 90 percent of the time, rips the package open and takes a huge bite from the top. He doesn't even snap off one of the four sticks like any normal, decent person would do. No, he bites a quarter off the top, so now all the bars have a chunk out of them. "Damn, that's good."

My mouth is open wide in shock. "I can't believe you just did that."

"What?"

"First of all, I was just telling Jess I'm saving it for a special occasion. I only have one white chocolate, and you...you...you..." I can't even express how pissed I am at him.

Nathan shrugs, then holds out the rest of the uneaten bar. "Here, you want a bite?"

Yuck! "You bit off the whole top. You're supposed to snap off the sticks one at a time. Everyone knows that. Now the entire thing is tainted with your saliva germs."

"Come on, Amy. You've been exposed to my saliva germs before." He makes a smooching noise, then grins. "So what's the big deal?"

I pretend to gag. "Don't remind me."

You probably think I hate Nathan. I don't. Next to Jessica, he's my best friend and the most entertaining thing I have in my life, especially when Avi and I are apart. Nathan is like my very own live Elmo doll that walks, talks, and farts. Maybe that isn't the greatest analogy, but you get the idea.

"I'll have a bite," Miranda sheepishly chimes in, leaning toward the half-eaten chocolate.

Nathan sticks his tongue out at me and moves the chocolate closer to Miranda. She takes a bite, then Nathan finishes it off by popping the rest in his mouth. Miranda can be my guest and swap germs with Nathan all she wants.

"You owe me another *Kif-Kaf*," I tell him. "A *white chocolate* one."

"Whatever," he says, licking his fingers one by one, making those little sucking sounds on each one to annoy me.

"Keep doin' that, big guy. You forget that my strong, military commando boyfriend will kick your butt once I tell him you mutilated my white Kit Kat without my permission."

Nathan stops licking his fingers. "Seriously, tell that guy to stay away from me. I think I still have bruise marks on my face in the shape of his fist."

"Avi only hit you because you attacked him first," I remind him.

"You told me to, Amy," Nathan says defensively. "You know, during your stupid Operation Get-Avi-Back on the Northwestern campus."

Nathan's right—but it was only to stall Avi so I could let him know I was devastated we broke up during his trip to Chicago. I was desperate to get back together. It wasn't a stupid plan. It was brilliant, especially because it worked. "Well, that's old news. Avi doesn't even remember you."

Okay, so that's not exactly true. Sometimes Avi will ask about Nathan when we talk on the phone. He knows Nathan and I kissed ... he doesn't know it was *three* times, though. To be completely honest, the first time was awful, the third time was fake (it was actually last month—to make his ex-girlfriend Bicky believe he was dating me so she'd stop dropping into his life), but the second time ...

I don't want to think about that second time. So Nathan knows how to kiss when he puts a little effort into it. It's not a big deal.

It doesn't matter, anyway. Avi is the only guy I ever want to kiss. He knows nearly everything about me (of course, he's never heard me on the toilet because I run the water when I'm in the bathroom, and he has no clue I have a fear of spiders), and the guy still loves me. My dad warns me not to wait around for him, because he's in Israel and we have a long-distance relationship. He also says we're too young to say we'll be together forever.

As if my dad knows about love. My dad is single and has just started dating Marla, the woman who runs the coffee shop in the building next to our condo. I admit I set them up ... one night I invited her over, and when my dad came home I had Nathan come up with an excuse to get me out of there so they could have some alone-time. The rest is history; at least, it will be when my dad decides to ask Marla to marry him. Then I won't have to worry that he'll be without a partner the rest of his life.

The bus comes to a stop and I glance out the window. The security checkpoint, the gates, and the soldiers in green military uniforms clue me in that we've finally arrived at the base. Almost everywhere you go in Israel, you see someone in a military uniform and most have a rifle strapped to their backs.

I've only been to Israel once before (although this will be my first time on a military base) and I'm already desensitized to seeing military personnel everywhere I go, from the mall (they check your purse before you go inside to make sure you're not carrying an illegal bomb or weapon) to tourist and religious sites. They even have a security guy stationed outside the grocery store. It's totally different back home in Chicago. While the abundance of military presence in Israel isn't what I'm used to, it makes me feel tremendously safe.

I'll have to remember to pray for the day Israelis don't have to worry about war or terrorism. I also have to pray they can make some sort of peace with their neighbors, because I'm a huge "let's make love, not war" kind of person.

Speaking of love...I look out the window and crane my neck to see if I can spot Avi. No such luck.

Pulling out my makeup case, I tell Jess to hold up the mirror so I can brush on more blush and fix any smudged eyeliner. Then I hold up the mirror for Jess so she can do the same.

"What are you girls doing?" Nathan asks, laughing.

"Fixing ourselves."

"This isn't a beauty pageant, you know. It's the IDF."

"We know," Jess says, dipping the lip gloss applicator in the tube and applying it to her lips. "But who says just because you're in the army you have to look like crap?"

"Seriously, Nathan. Don't you know anything about girls?"

"Apparently not." He turns to Miranda and puts his hands in a praying position. "Don't be like them, okay?"

"I like the way they look," Miranda tells him. "If I was as pretty as them, I'd do the same."

He slaps his palm against his forehead. "I cannot believe what I'm hearing. Miranda, you're fine as-is." *Great, Nathan, treat her as if she's a defective as-is item sold on the clearance rack.*

"Miranda, I need makeup to look good," I tell her. "You're naturally pretty."

When the bus passes through the checkpoint, my heart starts racing. I wonder when we'll have free time to explore the base so I can search for Avi.

"Don't volunteer for anything," a guy in the seat behind us whispers through the space between the seats. "Pass it down."

I pass the message down.

"I heard if you volunteer, you'll be stuck doing some crappy assignment," Jess says.

Note taken. I will not volunteer. I have a major aversion to crappy assignments.

2

Why couldn't God have given humans doggie sweat glands, so we could gracefully pant our sweat away?

Our military leaders, or *ha'mefa'ked* in Hebrew (if you say it fast it sounds like *I'm a [insert cuss word]*), are named Ronit and Susu. They're both Israeli, both in the military, and *their* crappy assignment is being in charge of us during boot camp. Susu is in charge of the twenty guys and Ronit is in charge of the twenty girls.

Ronit stands next to the bus driver with her clipboard in hand. "Girls, please find your suitcases and follow me to the *bittan*. Boys, follow Susu."

We gather our backpacks and file off the bus.

"If they're gonna separate the guys from the girls, can we at least have co-ed showers?" Nathan mumbles.

"You're a pig," I tell him.

"Shh, don't say the word 'pig' so loud, Amy," Nathan whispers in my ear. "Pigs aren't kosher, you know."

"Whatever, Nathan. It's not like I'm gonna eat it. I just *said* it."

Some of the stronger American guys from our trip are unloading our luggage. I would be searching for my luggage, but I'm too consumed with Avi-scanning and fanning my face with my hand because it's so hot outside.

You'd think God's holy land wouldn't be as hot as hell, but it is.

"Find your luggage fast, ladies!" Ronit's voice booms from behind us. "And follow me!"

"Does she have to be so cheery all the time?" Jess asks. "It's irritating."

"Maybe she loves her job," Miranda chimes in.

I snort, on purpose. "Maybe she's got a personality disorder."

I watch as Nathan joins the other guys following Susu. I have to give major credit to Nathan for always fitting in as "one of the guys." He's never an outcast or out of place, because everyone likes him. It's a trait that totally annoys someone like me—I only feel comfortable with people who know me.

I spot my hot pink luggage that I bought for my trip. One big rolling suitcase and one smaller one. My father wanted me to buy a dorky duffel or some boring luggage that had been "rated highly" (my dad's words, not mine) by Consumer Reports, but I'd axed that suggestion because the only colors available were *black* and *black with dark gray trim*. I have one word to describe them: BOR-ING!

I want my luggage to reflect my personality. And I'm anything *but* boring. I pull out the handles to my girlie suitcases and start wheeling them away from the others.

Ronit holds her hand high in the air and says, "Follow me, girls!" as she heads down the road. "*Yala, zooz*! Hurry!"

Most of the girls in our group are lugging duffels (okay, I admit the brochure might have recommended them, but it'd be impossible to shove all my stuff in a duffel ... and I'd never be able to carry it even if I could). How these girls can fit their necessities into one bag is beyond me.

Miranda, Jessica, and I are lagging behind. I mean, come on ... who can hurry when it's so damn hot outside? Jessica has two pink suitcases, just like me, but hers have huge rhinestone/diamond studs spelling out JESSICA across the side. Miranda only has one painfully boring black suitcase. The poor girl is sweating so much there are wet spots in the shape of half-moons under her boobs.

"I think I'm going to die," Miranda says, yanking a portable fan out of her suitcase and hanging it around her neck. "Where are the barracks?"

I would feel sorry for her, except my boobs have the same half-moon wet spots and I don't have a portable fan.

3

*Everything from your sunglasses to your suitcase should
reflect your unique style and attitude.*

With my designer sunglasses protecting my eyes, my backpack on my back, and a suitcase rolling in each hand, I'm
walking slowly down the road. We're passing offices and off-
white buildings made out of cement. I'm painfully aware
of the many Israeli soldiers pointing to the three of us and
snickering.

*Yes, gawk at the American girls struggling with their lug-
gage,* I want to say, but don't. We must look totally out
of place with our Abercrombie outfits and pimped-out
suitcases. Listen, I don't blame them for laughing. I'm definitely out of my element.

I silently pray for Avi to come to my rescue and take
my luggage to the barracks for me.

Sweat rolls down my forehead. Where is my boyfriend? And how big is this army base anyway?

"Come on, girls!" Ronit urges from far down the road.

Jess puts on a huge fake smile and waves to our leader. "We're coming!" she says, mimicking Ronit's cheery tone. Jess and I know she's making fun of Ronit, but I doubt anyone else does. "Don't they have a bellman?" She wipes her upper lip that's beading with sweat. "They better have air-conditioned rooms. I just got my lip waxed and don't have anything for the sweat to cling to."

"Ugh, TMI," I tell her.

"It's true, Amy. Do you have another portable fan with you, Miranda?"

She shakes her head.

I look left and right to see if I can catch a glimpse of my boyfriend. "Avi has got to be around here somewhere, right?"

Jess sighs. She misses Tarik, her boyfriend. He's Palestinian, and although he's not thrilled about her spending part of her summer on an Israeli military base, he understands her commitment to her religion because he feels the same about his.

Jessica is Jewish and Tarik is Muslim. You'd think they'd avoid each other like I avoid political debates, but ever since they met they've chosen to ignore the obvious obstacles in their relationship. So who am I to bring it up? I'm a huge fan of living in ignorant bliss.

I'm wondering when this lugging-luggage torture will

be over. My suitcases are kicking up dust from the gravel road. Now I'm not only sweaty, but dirty too. I pull harder. Visions of a hot shower with my papaya-scented bath gel and a nice relaxing nap on a featherbed dance in my brain.

Suddenly, I hear a snap and watch one of the wheels on my beautiful, designer, hot-pink suitcase roll away from me and bounce to the bottom of a ditch. I suck in a horrified breath.

4

It boggles my mind that there's a direct correlation
between lack of quality and bling.
At least in the suitcase department.

"Whoa, that sucks," Jess says slowly.

Miranda points to the offending wheel. "Amy, is that yours?"

"Yep." So now I have a broken piece of luggage and I'm still not at our barracks.

I swallow my ego and start walking toward the stupid broken wheel. I eye it in the ditch where it stopped. I'm wearing a pink tank and white jean shorts, and I know if I slip as I go down I'm going to have dirt all over me. Oh, don't go blaming me about wearing white shorts... climbing down into a ditch to retrieve a stupid wheel wasn't exactly one of the warnings in the *Sababa* brochure.

I take one step down. My foot slides a little, then stops.

I probably should tell you now that I'm wearing these really cute pink mules that aren't really made for traction—but they sure do match my tank perfectly. I'm not about to take out the gym shoes I bought for this trip, because they're at the bottom of one of my suitcases.

I take another step, and wobble because I'm walking on an angle.

"Be careful," Miranda warns.

Before I take another step, a boy in uniform walks up to us. "*Mah karah?*" he asks. He's got short hair and beautiful olive skin without a trace of acne.

"*Angleet, b'vakashah,*" I say. My dad taught me that phrase, which means "English, please."

"You need help?" He has a big Israeli accent along with a big Israeli smile (he's also got a big Israeli rifle slung on his back).

"Desperately," I admit, pointing to the wheel.

He scrambles down the bank as if he does it every day of his life, and picks up the wheel. On his way back up, he grabs my elbow and helps me back to the gravel road. Then attempts to reattach the wheel.

"This suitcase is a piece of *sheet,*" he informs me. "It can't be fixed." He hands me the plastic wheel. I almost laugh at the word "sheet"—American profanity with an Israeli accent comes out really funny. But I'm sweaty and unhappy and cannot physically laugh right now.

I shove the wheel in the front pocket of my suitcase. "Well, thanks for trying."

"Yeah, thanks," Miranda chimes in.

The guy holds out his hand. "I'm Nimrod."

"No, really, what's your name?" I ask.

"Nimrod."

He did not just say *Nimrod*, did he? With the Israeli accent it sounds like *Nim-road*.

I put my sunglasses on top of my head, eyeing him suspiciously. "*Nimrod?*"

"Nimrod. I guess in America this is not a popular name, no?"

Jess is trying not to laugh. Miranda just looks confused. Some names in Israel do not translate to English well. Avi has friends named Doo-Doo, Moron, and O'dead. And my cousin's name is pronounced O'snot.

"I'm Amy. And this is Jessica and Miranda," I say, pointing to each of my friends.

Nimrod heaves the entire suitcase up into his arms. "Your group is at the *bittan* on the other side of the hill. I'll help you."

"Thanks," I say, noting that my hot pink suitcase looks very out of place in Nimrod's arms and I still have no clue what a *bittan* is. I roll my smaller suitcase behind him. As we pass other soldiers, they make comments in Hebrew to Nimrod, who laughs and shrugs as he leads us up the hill.

The guy isn't breaking a sweat in this heat, which is not normal. Looking around, I notice that none of the Israeli soldiers milling around are sweating. It makes me wonder if Israelis are born without sweat glands.

"Where are you girls from?" Nimrod asks.

"Chicago," I say.

"I've never been there, but there's a guy in my unit whose girlfriend lives there."

Could Nimrod know Avi? That would be so cool and easy if the first guy I meet on the base knows where Avi is. "Is his name Avi Gefen? Because I know he's stationed on this base for a few weeks this summer—"

Nimrod stops and his eyes bug out. "*You're* Gefen's girlfriend?"

I smile wide. I can't help it. "Yep."

I think I notice the corners of his mouth twitch, but I'm not sure. "Does Gefen know you're here?"

"No," I say sheepishly. "It's kind of a surprise."

"Oh, he will *definitely* be surprised." We all follow Nimrod to what I assume is the barracks (aka *bittan*). I spot them now. The barracks are off-white cement buildings (similar to every building on base), but they're one story and have only two small windows on each side.

"Amy! Jessica! Miranda!"

I wince at the sound of Ronit's voice. The four of us reach our very annoyed leader. She's standing next to a guy who resembles a Russian boxer I once saw in an old Rocky movie...or a WWE wrestler. He's over six feet tall with blond hair and blue eyes. And his arms are crossed on his chest, making his huge muscles bunch up. Avi's muscles are huge, but this guy must weightlift small cars to get his arms that bulky.

I point to the luggage in Nimrod's hand. "Sorry we lagged behind. One of my suitcases broke."

Nimrod sets my luggage down and salutes to the big, blond wrestler.

"Girls, this is Sergeant Ben-Shimon," Ronit says, introducing us to the big dude. "He'll be your unit commander."

"Oh, cool," I say. "Can we just call you Sergeant Ben?"

"No," he says in a stern voice. "The rest of your unit is already having lunch."

Great, they all left without us. "Well, I guess if you point us in the direction of the mess hall or whatever you call the place where we eat, that'll be great."

Ronit points to the open doorway. "Put your suitcases in the *bittan*, then follow me to the *cheder ochel*, where soldiers eat. There isn't much time left before your next activity."

The inside of the place we'll be sleeping for the next three weeks isn't pretty. Bunk beds are lined up in neat rows (just in case you were wondering, the bunks are made out of metal, not wood) and the mattresses don't resemble anything like featherbeds. The place is not air conditioned, and the windows are open. Unfortunately, the door to the room is open to the outside, too, so a few bees are flying around.

Do the *Sababa* tour people know that sleeping with bees is so *not sababa*?

Jessica and I eye each other. We don't even have to talk, because we've been best friends long enough to know what the other is thinking.

Miranda says, "This isn't so bad."

Jessica and I don't answer.

We all set our suitcases inside the barracks, then follow Ronit.

"Where are the bathrooms?" I ask. "I had an entire Diet Coke on the bus and I've got to pee."

"Me, too," Jessica says.

Miranda admits she's been holding it for the past two hours, so Ronit leads us to a small structure. It's bigger than a port-a-potty but smaller than the girls' bathroom at Chicago Academy, where I go to school.

"Here. But you better hurry, girls."

We file inside the bathroom. The stench of pee/poo/bacterial disinfectant creeps up my nostrils immediately.

Jess takes her designer sunglasses off her nose slowly. "This place stinks so bad my eyes are starting to water."

I plug my nose. "Seriously, Mutt's farts aren't this bad." (Mutt is my crazy dog, and yes, he is a mutt.)

I hurry to pull back a curtain, which I assume is the equivalent to a bathroom stall back home. When I peek at what's behind the curtain, I can't believe my eyes.

It's a hole. In the ground.

Okay, so that's not entirely the right way to describe it.

It's a hole in the ground with two rubber non-skid mats in the shape of feet on either side of it ... I guess for dumb people who have no clue where to place their feet.

"I can't pee in that," I say, but saying the word 'pee' makes my urge to do it that much stronger.

Jess whines. "Do you think I can hold it in for two weeks?"

I look back at Ronit. "Do you have any bathrooms with toilets?"

"This *is* a bathroom. And that's a toilet."

"No, that's a hole."

Ronit was previously cheery, but I think we've cracked her and now she's bordering on annoyed. She steps forward. "This isn't a hotel or spa, ladies. It's the IDF. Now either pee or not, I don't care. But you have three minutes to do your business and head to the *cheder ochel* to eat, or you'll be finding yourselves assigned to bathroom cleaning duties."

With that, Ronit leaves the three of us alone.

"I hate her," Jess says.

Miranda's mouth starts to quiver. I'm not sure if it's because she's late for lunch or because she doesn't know how to pee in a hole.

"My bladder is about to burst," I say, pushing past Jessica and closing the curtain shut.

"I'll go in the one next to you," Jess says.

I notice the graffiti on the side wall. In pen, someone etched words in English. It says: *Beware of the Loof!*

What or *who* is the Loof?

I don't have time to think about the Loof too hard. I put my feet on the rubber pads and pull down my shorts. But when I try and squat, they're in the way.

"I can't squat for this long," Jess says. "My thigh muscles are starting to quiver."

"I think I just peed on my leg," Miranda informs us. Eww!

When I'm finally in position, I can't relax because I'm listening to my two friends complain. "Shut up, guys. My pee is getting stage fright from listening to you both yapping."

"Thirty seconds!" Ronit yells from outside.

Yeah, as if pressure is going to help me relax.

I hear Miranda wash her hands and head outside. Then I hear Jess washing her hands by the sink. "Hurry up, Amy," she whispers loudly. "I don't want to do doo-doo duty."

I look down at the hole, to see if I am aiming in the right spot. "Oh, shit!" I yell. "My sunglasses fell in the hole!" I forgot they were on top of my head!

"If you stick your hand down there to get them, I cannot be best friends with you anymore. Just leave them!" Jess calls out. "And hurry up!"

"Those cost me $235."

"Now they're worth nothing. Come on!"

For a nanosecond I contemplate fishing them out of the crap (literally) below, but . . . I just can't. I think if I did I'd require more therapy than I already need.

Wiping myself (with brown toilet paper resembling brown paper towels they have in the art room at school—which I now know is very scratchy and irritating on sensitive body parts) and putting my undies and shorts back on, I pray that I see Avi soon. Because this army experience is not me, and while I knew that the experience would be challenging, I also knew that seeing Avi for even a little bit would be worth it.

Now if I could just find my boyfriend . . .

5

Lunch was in a hot and sweaty coed building. Well, to be specific, I was hot and sweaty... the room was just hot. I caught a glimpse of Nathan, who seemed to be entertaining his table because everyone was focused on him. The meal consisted of overcooked chicken (considering I only eat white meat and came to lunch late, I was stuck eating legs and thighs), yellow rice, and a pea/mushroom concoction. Drinks were a choice of room-temperature tap water or room-temperature tap water (you guessed it, there wasn't a choice at all). And I'm not sure Israelis know what ice is, because every time I asked for it they got a confused look on their face.

Oh, yeah. They had hot coffee and hot tea as drink

alternatives, but I don't drink those and anyway who in their right mind would want a hot beverage when it feels like it's a hundred degrees outside? There wasn't even a Coke machine.

At the end of our hurried meal, we all place our garbage in cans and the plates/silverware in plastic bins, and are instructed to line up outside in neat rows.

Someone taps me on the shoulder. I turn around, hoping against all hope that it's Avi, but it's not. "Oh, it's you."

Nathan puts his arm around me. "Oh, come on. Admit that you missed me."

"We've only been apart for a little more than an hour, Nathan. Give me time to miss you." I shrug his arm off me. "I see you've made friends already."

"The guys in my unit are cool, but I'd rather bunk with you girls," he says as we line up with the others like good little soldiers. For over twenty minutes we're taught how to get in formation. Five rows of eight people each, an arm's length apart. "At ease" is hands behind your back with your legs spread shoulder width apart. "Attention" is saluting with your feet together.

Ronit is standing in front of the entire group, with Sergeant "Don't-Call-Me-Ben"-Shimon next to her.

"Let's just say I'm glad you're on the other side of the base," I whisper to Nathan as the sergeant starts talking.

"I can always sneak out with the guys and peek in on you girls while you're changing," he whispers back.

I wish I could talk louder but everyone is quiet, listening to the sergeant. I'll have to get briefed later on what he's saying, because I'm not listening. Instead, I whisper, "Nathan, you're a perv."

"We can call it Operation Boobie Watch," he whispers back, but emphasizes the word "boobie," which he knows I hate. *Boobage, boobie, jugs, hammocks*, etc … I hate all the nicknames for boobs.

Operation Boobie Watch? Eww! I know Nathan doesn't mean it. He's just trying to get a rise out of me because it entertains him. He knows how to push my buttons … especially when it comes to boobs.

God gave me this body, but I really wish he'd have given me less of it in the boob department.

In response to Nathan's comment, I shove him away from me. Which isn't the best idea in the world, because now Sergeant "Don't-Call-Me-Ben"-Shimon stops talking and focuses his ice-blue eyes on us.

"Tell me your names?"

Everyone is staring at us. We're in big trouble. Oh, crap. "Amy," I squeak out. Guess he didn't remember we already were introduced by the barracks.

"Nathan, sir!" I hear from my best guy friend/enemy/annoyance beside me. He says it loud and clear, like he's been in the military his entire life instead of just one and a half hours.

"Amy, what was I just explaining?" the sergeant asks me.

Double oh-crap. I dare not tell the guy I was expecting

to get the shortened version by asking my friends. Deciding there's no other way around it, I tell him the truth.

"I don't know…SIR!" I figure adding the 'sir' might earn *me* some brownie points—it seemed to work for Nathan. But from the sergeant's eyebrow-furrowing expression, I realize my 'sir' didn't work.

He stands in front of Nathan and asks the same question. Nathan's response is the same as mine.

"You and you," the sergeant says, pointing to each of us. "Follow me."

We follow the guy to the front of the entire American trainee unit. Looking ahead, I see Jessica with a worried expression. She knows I'm not into the whole military thing.

"Give me twenty," the sergeant commands, with his hands on his hips.

"You mean like dollars?" I ask. "Or shekels? I mean, I left my purse back in my suitcase."

Nathan nudges me. "He means pushups, Amy. Not money."

Oh. Right. "I knew that," I lie. I'm sorry if when someone says "give me twenty" my mind doesn't automatically think of physical activity.

Nathan flashes me a "loser" sign on his forehead.

The sergeant points to us, then the ground.

Nathan gets into position on the ground, supporting himself by his toes and hands.

"Can I do it the girlie way?" I ask. "Our gym teacher

Mr. Haraldson lets us." When the sergeant looks confused I add, "You know, with my knees on the ground."

"Fine."

I get in position next to Nathan, knowing my white shorts are now beyond repair. When Nathan starts, I start. My knees are on gravel, and rocks are digging into my skin.

After I do one pushup, sweat drips off my forehead and lands on the gravel beneath me. I do a few more, then stop to look over at Nathan. He's groaning after a few minutes and lies down on the dirt exhausted and sweaty like me.

"You both are weak. Get up."

The sergeant has Nathan and me stand side by side in front of everyone. "*Small* is left, *ya'mean* is right. When I say *small*, you march with your left foot. When I say *ya'mean*, you march with your right foot. Understand?"

Nathan says, "Yes, sir!" like a total kiss-ass army recruit.

I raise my hand. "Excuse me, I have a question."

The sergeant looks at me as if I'm the stupidest person on earth. Sure, when it comes to marching I might lack the basic natural instincts. But get me on my own turf and I know all there is to know about the city and how to maneuver in it. Some people call Chicago a jungle, but it's my jungle and my turf.

I'm not used to this military jungle, though.

"What *zee* problem?" he says impatiently. It's weird—when Israelis get upset their accent gets more pronounced. I know that from my dad, because he's Israeli.

Everyone is still watching, which makes me nervous. I even hear a few snickers from the American guys. Remind me to listen to every single syllable Sergeant "Don't-Call-Me-Ben"-Shimon (from now on referred to as Sergeant B-S) says from this second forward. I don't want to be put front and center again.

The sun is glaring in my eyes. I squint up at the sergeant and silently curse the poop hole I dropped my sunglasses in. "Yeah, I was um ... I was wondering if you lift your foot on the *smalls* and *ya'means* or if you put your foot down on them. Could you clarify, please?"

"You put your foot down on them," my boyfriend's voice says from behind me.

6

Avoid public humiliation at all costs—
especially in front of your boyfriend.

I whirl around to see Avi. He's a few yards away, walking toward me. His face is tan and his profile is chiseled like a Roman statue. His hair is a little grown out from his buzz cut. He's so hot and sexy I can't help but stare in awe at my boyfriend who professed his love to me in letters (yes, he actually sits down and writes actual letters to me when he can't call), and in voicemail messages he left when he visited me in Chicago. I've saved them all and listen to them every time I need to hear his voice. Not being able to hold myself still any longer, I catapult forward and wrap my arms around his neck.

"Avi!" I cry into his chest. "Are you surprised?"

"Very." He gently takes my wrists and unwinds them

from around his neck. He salutes the sergeant, who says something in Hebrew. Avi answers.

So this is a time when I wish I knew Hebrew. I take Spanish. A few months ago I told my dad to stop speaking to me in English and only speak to me in Hebrew. That lasted about an hour, because I wanted to rip my hair out from not understanding him and got annoyed by his hand gestures when he pointed to objects, trying to give me hints. I wanted to learn Hebrew, not play charades.

Avi looks down at me. "We can't talk now."

Beside me, Nathan is tense. The last time I was reunited with Avi, back in January when he came to Chicago, he'd caught Nathan with his arm around my shoulders. It was not a happy time in our relationship, especially when Avi found out a few days later that Nathan and I had kissed in the cafeteria at school in front of half of the Chicago Academy student body.

But that was a long time ago. I'm here in Israel now, standing in front of my boyfriend who's in the Israeli military until he's at least twenty-one. Avi is wearing a sand-colored uniform, unlike most of the soldiers on the base who are wearing olive green. All of us Americans are still in our regular clothes, so we look out of place among the real soldiers.

"I know we can't talk right this second," I tell Avi. "But after I learn how to do the marching thing, do you have any free time so we can be alone? Just you and me."

"Amy, we can't go anywhere alone. It's against base rules."

"But I'm your *girlfriend*, not some *random*."

I hear snickers behind Avi. Leaning so I can see who's behind him, I notice Nimrod standing with four guys and a girl all in sand-colored uniforms like Avi's. The girl is covering her mouth to suppress her giggle. She's not wearing a stitch of makeup on her perfectly flawless skin, has long sandy blond hair with natural streaks in it tied up in a ponytail, and is really tall. To add insult to injury, she's got normal-sized, perfect boobs. I bet they stand at attention without a bra, while (as my mother always reminds me) God blessed me with boobs that need a little help being lifted.

I feel like an ogre next to this Israeli girl.

I would give her my famous sneer, but she's got a rifle so I figure it's in my best interest not to piss her off. I then notice they all have big rifles strapped to their backs. Avi does too.

Guns scare me. Especially big ones with bullets in them.

"Attention!" Sergeant B-S barks at me. I stand next to Nathan with my hands stiffly at my sides. We're still in front of everyone, so I guess our punishment for talking isn't over. This sucks.

The sergeant says something to Avi and his posse, then they all stand back and watch. "Ready," the sergeant says to Nathan and me. It's not a question.

Ready or not, I'm about to march. In front of the rest of my unit, and in front of Avi and his friends.

"*Small. Small. Small-ya'mean-small. Small. Small. Small-ya'mean-small.*" Nathan and I follow the sergeant as we demonstrate how to march. I'm all too aware of Avi's gaze on me, and I want to die from embarrassment because I'm royally screwing up. I'm *smalling* on the *ya'means* and *ya'meaning* on the *smalls*. It's not that I'm uncoordinated. I'm just nervous.

Glancing sideways, I catch sight of Avi. I can't tell what he's thinking because he's got a composed, soldier-like expression.

As my eyes meet Avi's, I stumble into the sergeant, who must have stopped and barked stopping orders while I was still *smalling* and *ya'meaning*. "Oops," I say as my nose bumps his back. Actually, my boobs bumped him first because they're a gazillion times bigger than my nose, but I hope nobody noticed.

"*B'amakom atz'or* means you stop." Ronit clues me in.

"Got it. Thanks." I salute her because I want to be all military-like, but the saluting just brings more snickers from Avi's friends until he glares at them.

Oh, God, I hope he's not ashamed of me. What if his feelings for me changed since he came to visit back in January? What if he likes the gorgeous streaked-blond girl with the big rifle?

That very girl whispers to my boyfriend, then looks in my direction. Avi nods. Our eyes meet again, and I wish I could speak telepathically. But he just keeps up that stern military expression. It's driving me nuts.

I've seen Avi smile and laugh. I've *made* Avi smile and laugh.

Ronit calls out, "Girls, follow me! Guys, follow Susu!"

While we're scrambling to obey, Avi is at my side. The warmth of his fingers on my elbow sends shivers down my spine.

"What are you doing here?" he asks me. "I thought you were staying on the *moshav* with your dad."

"I was. Until I realized Jess and Miranda and Nathan were going to be on the same base as you. I thought you'd be happy to see me. Obviously I was wrong."

"Gefen, *zooz*," the sergeant barks out.

Avi turns his head to the sergeant, who doesn't look happy that Avi's talking to me. "I gotta go."

"So go," I say sarcastically. Okay, I know I'm acting like a complete brat but seriously... I came all the way to Israel and signed up to play soldier for ten days just to be with him, and he doesn't seem the least bit excited to see me.

"Amy..." he says, but I shrug his hand off me.

"Go," I repeat.

He sighs and walks away.

7

Israel is .004% of the earth's surface.
They say the most valuable things come
in small packages.

So now I'm depressed and want to go home. Seeing Avi in all his military splendor grilling me on why I came here wasn't exactly how I imagined it. I'm sluggish as I follow the girls inside a building and we all sit in chairs in a classroom. To my surprise, the snickering girl from Avi's unit came with us and is obviously about to teach us something.

"This is Liron," Ronit explains. "She's one of the few female operations specialists assigned to a new IDF commando unit called Sayeret Tzefa. They've just come back from parachute training and are spending a few weeks on our base before they head off to Counter Terror School. We're very lucky to have them here to train you."

The other girls are immediately impressed by Liron. Even though she's not an official member of Sayeret Tzefa, by working alongside it she's as close as a female can get. We spend the next two hours listening to her talk about the state of Israel and the countries that surround it.

"Who can tell me why Israel is so significant?" she asks.

I definitely know why it's significant to me, especially since for the past year I've been taking conversion classes at my synagogue. My mom raised me with no religion, and my dad is Jewish. Last summer when I came to Israel, I connected with my Jewish heritage and wanted to learn all I could about it.

I raise my hand along with a couple of the other girls, totally ignoring the fact that my sweaty armpits smell like rotten eggs.

"You, in the pink tank top," Liron says, pointing to me. "Your name is Amy, right? Avi's *chaverah*."

"His girlfriend," I clarify.

"*Chaverah* means girlfriend."

"I knew that."

Liron smiles at me, and I notice not only is her skin flawless, but her teeth are perfectly straight. "So Amy, why do you think Israel is significant?"

I sit up straight in my hot metal chair, which my thighs have stuck to from the heat. My skin rubs on the metal with each movement, making a squeaking sound. It hurts. I'll probably have thigh-burn later on. "Because it's the Jewish homeland," I answer.

Liron nods. "You're right. As Americans, you share the same democratic freedoms we do here in Israel."

"The Palestinians don't have it so easy here," Jess chimes in. "I mean, I'm proud to be Jewish and would never want to be anything else, but when will the fighting stop?"

Oh, no! While Tarik would be proud of Jess for sticking up for his people, I'm not sure this is the best place to debate the Palestinian/Israeli conflict. And while I am usually all for a knock-down-drag-out verbal sparring session, I'm not sure anything but trouble can come out of a political discussion on an Israeli military base.

I decide to intervene. "I think my friend Jess here is trying to say that, uh, while Israel is the Jewish homeland, not everyone feels the same way. No need to go into the specific differences, though. It's all cool. Discussion over."

Liron walks down the aisle and stands in front of my chair. "It's against regulation for a soldier to talk about the political situation in Israel while in an IDF uniform. But I guarantee that you can get into a long political discussion with any Israeli out of uniform. And I also guarantee that you'll get a hundred and fifty different opinions if you talk to a hundred Israelis."

Whoa, that's a lot of opinions.

"Girls, my job in the IDF is to protect Israel. As a private, or new trainee, *your* job is to take orders. You will be treated like a real Israeli soldier, and you will act like a real Israeli soldier. When we say 'get in formation,' you get in formation or you'll be doing twenty pushups. When we say 'run,' you run. When we wake you at the crack of dawn, you'll be ready and in formation within seven minutes. We're going to test your will and your spirit. We're going to test you physically and mentally. You're going to hate and curse your instructors while you're going through it, and love us and feel like a stronger person in the end. Any questions?"

I raise my hand. When Liron points to me, I say, "Do we get free time?"

"Maybe," she answers curtly. "Why are you here, Amy?"

To spend time with my boyfriend, so Israeli girls like you don't steal him away from me, I want to say. But instead I say, "To feel what it's like to be an Israeli soldier."

An instructor named Gili comes in and talks to us about the state of Israel. "Israel has a population of about six million Jews," she explains. "We are a minority in the Middle East. It's no secret we cannot afford to lose even one war. To do so might mean the end of the state of Israel. That's why every single Jewish Israeli citizen must serve in the military. Israeli Druze and Bedouins serve in our military as well."

For the next two hours, Liron and other instructors take turns teaching us. I haven't paid much attention to the other girls in my unit, but being in a small classroom gives me the opportunity to check them out.

During the bus ride to the base, I learned that five of the girls are friends from New York. They all have straight brown hair and the same basic "look." They're taking this whole boot camp thing seriously and are determined to be obedient soldiers. I swear these New York girls can't wait to get down and dirty in the Israeli dirt. I think they're under the impression that at the end of our military basic training program they'll be ready for the front lines of battle. I don't have the heart to tell them they've got a demented view of reality.

We have four girls from California. They're all really pretty and two of them are fakey-blond.

Then there's Tori, our resident bitch. She's a total loner, by choice. She rolls her eyes at everything, and makes snide comments to just about everyone on the trip. I think her goal in life is to insult every person she comes in contact with. Her hair is long and blond, but when she turns around and her hair parts you can see that underneath she has a sheath of black hair. It's totally two-tone, but I have no clue if she wants it that way or if it's a bad dye job. Either way, it's definitely unique.

The rest of the seven girls in our barracks are from different states scattered around the country, although two are actually from Canada and I want to laugh every time they say the word "about" because it comes out as "ah-boot."

Right now we're being dismissed from the classroom. How can I break it to Ronit that I'm "ah-boot" to go search for my boyfriend?

8

Breaking the rules feels great while you're breaking them,
but horrible while you're paying for them.

Getting free time here is proving to be nearly impossible. After our classroom discussion, we're led back to our *bittan* and are instructed to pick a bunk and unpack. This is also a bathroom break time, but I'm not going in that place again until I absolutely have to. There really isn't unpacking to do because each of us only has a little cubby to put our stuff in—just big enough to fit my shampoo, conditioner, and makeup bag. I'll just have to live out of my suitcases while I'm here.

Because Jess, Miranda, and I got to the *bittan* late, Jess and I can't share a bunk. I sit on an unoccupied one.

"That's mine," Tori says, standing over me. "I called it first. You can have the top bunk."

I look around for an empty bottom bunk, but there aren't any left.

"That's fine," I say to Tori, who seems pretty pleased to boss me around. I would argue that I didn't hear her "call it first" or that I'm afraid of heights and I'll probably fall off the top bunk while I sleep, but all I want to do is find Avi. I couldn't care less about Tori and her bottom bunk.

Just when I think free time has begun, it's time for the next activity. Ronit hands out pillows, sheets, and a very thin wool blanket. For the next hour, she teaches us how to make our beds. We have to keep unsheeting and re-sheeting until we get the A-okay from Ronit that we've finally done it to IDF standards (picture tight hospital corners). I can tell you right now that making tight hospital corners on a top bunk is tons harder than on a bottom bunk.

My bunk is two away from Miranda's and across from Jessica's. I can tell it'll be close to impossible to have private late-night chats.

"Everyone line up outside!" Ronit yells. "*Yala, zooz!*"

I don't exactly know what "*Yala, zooz*" means, but from her tone I guess it means "Come on, hurry up." I have a feeling I'll be hearing those words a lot while I'm here.

Jess pulls me aside before we go. "Switch bunks with me," she says. "You want a bottom bunk, right?"

"Yeah, but—"

"Well, it's right by the door so you can get fresh air." Jess is already bringing her stuff over to my cubby and switching my stuff out. "Just do it. We've got to hurry and get out outside before they make us do pushups. I hate pushups."

Liron and Ronit time how long it takes until we're all in formation outside. Ronit walks in front of us like a lion pacing in her cage. "It took you fourteen minutes. I think that's the worst I've ever seen! Next time," she says, "you'll do it in half the time—seven minutes. And then we'll cut it to three. March in formation to the *cheder ochel* for dinner! Ready?" she barks out.

She must not expect us to respond, because immediately she starts chanting the *small-ya'mean-smalls*. We're all out of line and out of sequence, bumping into each other. Ronit stops us. She makes us go back to the barracks each time we screw up until we get it right. The guys, who have obviously mastered marching in formation, have been gawking at us the entire time from the entrance to the *cheder ochel.*

We've attempted to get there six times. We're all getting crabby and tired. The seventh time, we're almost there when I spot Avi. He's standing by the American guys, watching me. I get so excited and nervous to see him that I totally screw up and step right on the back of Tori's foot, so hard that her shoe comes off.

"Stop!" Ronit says, then sighs in frustration. "Okay, girls. Back to the *bittan* for another try!"

Tori grabs her shoe. "What a *spaz*," she mutters.

Is she kidding me? "Oh, like you're so perfect with *your* marching?"

Tori flips her fake blond hair over her shoulder. "I've been dancing since I was five. I know how to count off."

I don't tell her that I've been dancing since I was four. I want to talk to Avi before he's whisked off so I ignore her. We line up again, and this time I look at the back of Tori's head so I don't mess up. In the end, it takes us thirty-five minutes to walk the three minutes to the *cheder ochel*.

On our way into the building, I look for Avi again. I spot him talking to other soldiers. While everyone rushes to stuff their faces with mediocre food, I walk up to my boyfriend. "Can we go somewhere private?"

"Amy, I can't."

"What? You can't talk to your girlfriend alone? You can't kiss your girlfriend you haven't seen for five months?"

"If someone catches us—"

"Let's go somewhere alone. For just a minute, Avi. *Please.*"

Before I even finish the word "please," Avi takes my hand and quickly whisks me away to a private alcove on the side of another building without windows. My mom says rules are made to be broken ... or at least stretched.

My stomach is in knots, and I tell myself not to be emotional. I'm also very aware that we could be in big trouble if we're caught.

But looking at Avi's face brings me back to the first day I met him. He was working at the sheep pens on the *moshav*, lugging bales of hay. I was afraid of the huge herding dogs running toward me so I leaped into the pens for safety. Instead of landing on the soft hay, I landed on Avi. He broke my fall. When I opened my eyes, I was staring into the most mesmerizing eyes I'd ever seen.

Being here with him, alone, makes me forget about rules and regulations. It's times like these I'm happy that I live in the gray areas of life. Being with Avi makes everything that's crappy in my life bearable.

I wrap my arms around his neck. This time he doesn't pull away. "I missed you so much," I say.

He raises his hand to my cheek and brushes his fingers softly down my face. For such a tough guy, Avi's touch has always been super gentle. "I can't resist you," he says softly.

I'm relieved and excited when his lips touch mine. I wrap my arms around his waist and try to ignore the feel of his rifle against my fingers. When I urge him closer, our kiss gets more heated. As soon as his tongue touches mine, my insides feel like hot, molten lava.

My emotions are running high and I know a tear has escaped from the corner of my eye.

He pulls away a little. "Don't cry."

With the back of my hand, I quickly wipe whatever tears have escaped. "I'm not," I tell him.

He hesitates. "We need to talk. Seriously."

"About what?"

"About you being here. You said you'd be staying at the *moshav*."

I'm not going to lie to him. What would be the point?

"I'm here to be with you. To see you. To spend time with you."

"This is the military, Amy. I can't spend time with you here like we did last summer. I'm a soldier now."

"Well, now I'm a soldier too. At least for a little while. And we're spending time together right now, aren't we?"

"*Ze'heruit* Gefen," Nimrod calls out, startling me. "*Ata holech al chevel dok.*"

"*Sababa*," Avi answers back, then says to me, "I can't do this."

"What did Nimrod just say?" I ask.

"He said I should watch out because I'm walking a thin line."

Nimrod frowns at us. Avi and I both stay silent, ignoring the warning, until Nimrod shrugs and walks away.

"What can't you do?" I finally answer. "Be specific."

Avi rakes his hand through his hair, even though in actuality he's just raking his hand over his growing-out buzz cut. He looks me straight in the eye and says, "I don't want you here."

I think my heart just dropped into the pit of my stomach. "Why not?"

A sound to our right makes Avi tense as he surveys the source of the noise. It's only an American guy from my unit on his way to the bathroom.

"I don't want to upset you, Amy, but ... I can't do my job when I have to check up on you, worry about you, or make sure you're okay," he explains when the guy is out of sight. "You're a distraction."

"And what about that Liron girl in your unit? She's a girl. Why aren't you worried or distracted by her?"

"She's not my girlfriend. You are. And she's Israeli—you're American."

"So if I was Israeli, you'd be fine with me being here?"

"If you were Israeli, you wouldn't have a choice. You'd be required to serve in the military. But you're American."

Yeah, technically. But... "My dad is Israeli, so that makes me half Israeli. And I'm Jewish. I've heard that every Jewish person can automatically get Israeli citizenship just because they're Jewish."

"But you're *not* Israeli, Amy. Tell me you're okay with trading in your designer sunglasses and designer clothes." He takes my hand in his and looks at my painted nails. "And your pink nails, for dirt buried under your fingernails."

I pull my hand away. "For your information, Avi, I don't even own designer sunglasses." Okay, so technically I owned them a few hours ago, before they fell into the pee/poop hole in the bathroom. But I'd rather die than admit that fact. "And even though I do have painted nails, and I'd rather be at the beach than learning how to march in formation," I continue, examining my nails and noticing a new chip in my polish on my index finger that I'll have to fix later, "I'm doing this for you... for us."

"Gefen!" a guy yells out. That guy just happens to be none other than Sergeant B-S.

Oh, no! We're totally busted!

Avi straightens and whirls around. "*Ken, Ha'mefa'ked!*" he says, then salutes to the sergeant.

Sergeant B-S barks out some command in Hebrew. Then he says, "Amy, go eat. Don't stop on your way there."

"It's my fault that Avi and I are alone," I tell Sergeant B-S. "I—"

Avi takes my elbow and gives it a gentle squeeze, cutting my explanation short. "Just do as he says. I would make that an order, because I'm a higher rank than you. But I know you better than to do that. So I'll say *please*."

"I'm sorry I got you in trouble," I tell Avi quickly, then run to the *cheder ochel*.

Once there, everyone is busy eating dinner. Miranda waves me over. "Amy, over here!" I sit next to her and she pushes a plate full of food at me. "Here. I got you food."

I don't feel like eating, but know I need my strength. I nibble on bread and choke down the Israeli salad (which doesn't have any lettuce—what's up with that? It's just tomatoes, cucumbers, and onions). Every second or two I glance at the door to see if Avi walks in. I wonder how much trouble he's in and wish we could have avoided getting caught altogether.

Five minutes later (which means I checked the front entrance about three hundred times), Avi walks in with the sergeant. Neither look happy.

Avi's gaze briefly meets mine before he sits with the rest of the Sayeret Tzefa squad.

"Where were you?" Tori says to me from the opposite side of the table.

"In the bathroom," I lie.

"Oh, really? Because I saw you go off with that Israeli guy you hugged this morning and I was worried. I mean, I know the rules state we can get kicked out of the program if we're caught fooling around."

"So *you* told the sergeant?"

"Oh, no. Actually I told Ronit I was worried something happened to you. Of course she *was* talking to Sergeant Ben-Shimon at the time." Tori puts her fingers to her lips and sucks in a breath. "I didn't get you in trouble, did I?"

I don't buy her fake concern for a second. I let out a big, hearty chuckle. "No."

Tori is officially a person I will never trust. The girl is as manipulative as this girl Roxanne at my school.

Tori now gestures in the direction of Avi's table. "How do you know him?"

"He's her boyfriend," Miranda informs her cheerily. "They've been dating for a year."

"Wow. A long-distance relationship?"

"Yep," I say.

"So are you guys exclusive or what?"

That's a tricky question. Avi and I agreed to have a don't ask/don't tell policy since we're apart for such long periods of time. If I go on a casual date, I'm not going to tell Avi. He's not going to tell me if he's been on one, either. Avi and I are boyfriend and girlfriend, but we're trying to be realistic about our relationship.

"He's not available, if that's what you're thinking," I say, more defensively than I mean to.

If they weren't aware of it previously, our entire table now knows I'm dating Avi. I try not to glance at him while we're eating, but I can't help it. A few times I catch him looking back at me, but as soon as we make eye contact he breaks it.

This is definitely not turning out the way I expected. Has coming here been a huge mistake?

After we're done eating and scrape our plates into the big garbage bins (that don't have liners so I'm not sure how they clean them), we're excused to our barracks. I try to linger, hoping to exchange a few words with Avi, but Ronit comes up to me with a big frown on her face.

"Amy?" she says.

"Yeah."

"Follow me."

9

---

*Is it any wonder the person who invented pushups hasn't
come forward to claim their invention?*

It's just me and Ronit walking away from everyone else. I
follow my instructor to an open area, beyond the barracks.
To my surprise, Avi and Sergeant B-S are waiting for us.
Avi is standing at attention.

"Stand next to Avi," Ronit orders.

I have to get Avi out of trouble. I'm the one who lives
in the gray areas of life, not Avi, so he shouldn't be reprimanded.

"We're very disappointed in both of you," Ronit says.

"It was my fault," I admit to our superiors. "I begged
him to talk to me in priv—"

The sergeant, with a very pissed-off look on his face
(which has just gone a dark shade of red resembling a very

red grape), cuts me off in a stern loud voice. "Do not speak until spoken to!"

"But he—"

"Die!" (I learned back in January that *die* means "stop, enough!" in Hebrew … because when Avi told my dog to "die" when it was sniffing his crotch, I thought he was being rude, but he was just giving a command.)

I cover my mouth with my hands to stop myself from accidentally opening my lips and getting myself or Avi into more trouble.

Sergeant B-S steps between Avi and me. He gives Avi an order in Hebrew, then says, "Gefen, *Kadima!*" Then the sergeant turns to me. "Your job is to watch him. Come," he says, placing me a few feet in front of my boyfriend so I'm facing him.

"Watch him?" I question.

"Yes. Just stand and watch."

I know if I protest it's going to give him another reason to yell at me.

Avi, the ever-obedient soldier, gets on the gravel ground and does a pushup, then stands and our eyes meet. He repeats the pushup/standing exercise a few more times, and each time he stands our eyes meet. We can't talk, so our eye contact is the only way to communicate with each other.

Avi's straight, direct eye contact with me is telling me that he's okay … he's strong and he's fine.

I'm feeling worse than guilty. I wonder when he'll get to stop.

Avi is still going strong after five minutes, even though his back must be bruised from the rifle strapped to him. His palms are probably raw and bleeding from the gravel, too, but he doesn't give any sign he's in pain.

I hate watching this. The day has started to cool off, but I'm sweating again. Every time he goes down for another pushup, I wince. When he comes up, I want to tell him I'm sorry and won't lure him away again. After ten minutes, I swallow back tears and give Sergeant B-S a pleading look. He's got his arms folded in front of him, and doesn't show any sign of planning to let Avi stop any time soon.

I know when Avi is in pain, even though by looking at him you couldn't tell. I know it because he stops looking directly at me when he stands between those push-ups. He's looking forward, but not at me... he's looking through me. He's in "the zone" and is a robot now. It's a miracle he hasn't thrown up his dinner. I sure feel like throwing up mine.

My stomach twists. I can't deal with the fact that I'm just standing here doing nothing. I can't follow the order just to watch Avi. I know Avi won't stop until the sergeant says to, even if he's in pain.

I get it. Break down the soldier until they understand rules are not to be broken. Ever. Or else. Avi and I cannot go away in private even if we're dating. He knew this, but I lured him to break the rules and he did.

In the army there are no gray areas. I was wrong to ask him to break the rules, and Avi is paying the price for listening to me.

The next time he stands, I mimic him like a mirror and get on the ground to do a pushup with him. I try and do a manly pushup without putting my knees on the ground, even though my arms have the strength of a spaghetti noodle.

Silently I pray to God to give me strength.

When Avi and I both stand, this time he looks right at me and is not in "the zone" anymore. He shakes his head just the slightest bit, telling me to stop mimicking him. But I won't. I did the crime; it's not fair that he's the only one doing the time. The sergeant wanted to make me feel guilty. It worked.

I am back on the ground again, doing another pushup. Little pebbles get stuck to my sweaty palms, and it makes me cringe imagining what Avi's palms must feel like. But I don't stop.

"Die!" Sergeant B-S says.

For a second, I think he's giving an order for both of us to die on the spot... maybe he'll just take his gun and shoot us both. A harsh punishment for disobeying orders, but this is the army so maybe anything goes.

But then I remember it means "stop." Avi and I immediately stand at ease.

"I told you watch him. You're not good with following directions," the sergeant tells me.

I don't know if I'm supposed to answer or not, so I stay silent.

"Gefen tells me you and him are, uh, together. Is this the truth?"

My eyes stay on Avi when I say, "Yes, sir."

"This is a problem. On this base, between parachute training and Counter Terror School, Sayeret Tzefa trainees are assigned as instructors for the American volunteers. Special Ops soldiers must obey rules or they get reassigned. Eighty percent of Sayeret Tzefa trainees flunk training. Gefen might get reassigned as a driver if he doesn't obey the rules. And Gefen would rather die than be a driver. *Nachon*, Gefen?"

Avi stands tall and says, "*Ken, Ha'mefa'ked!*"

"I understand," I say. "It won't happen again."

"I don't care what you do off base or when Gefen is out of uniform. On my base, he's my soldier. Amy, you are a civilian trainee, don't forget that. Israeli soldiers are not to go off in private with civilian trainees of the opposite sex. Understand?"

"*Ken*, sir," I say, using the Hebrew word for "yes." It's one of the few Hebrew words that I actually know how to use correctly.

"You're both dismissed," he says. "*Zooz.*"

Avi does an immediate about-face and jogs away as if he hasn't just pushed his body to the limit. I want to run after him and apologize. I itch to examine his palms and take away whatever pain and cuts and bruises he's endured because of me.

I'm mentally drained and want this day to end. Sergeant B-S disappears while Ronit and I walk to the barracks. When we get inside, I notice that everyone has two sets of military olive green uniforms lying on their bunk, matching floppy hats, and a canteen with a strap. Liron is passing out towels.

"Shower time," Ronit informs me. "Each of you has seven minutes to shower."

I stand next to my bunk and receive my towel. Quickly collecting my papaya-scented bath gel, my poofy sponge, my shampoo, conditioner, and other essentials, I follow everyone to the showers.

Thank goodness the showers are next to, not *in*, the same room as the stinky bathrooms. There are six curtained stalls on either side. When it's our turn, I take the one next to Jessica.

The cement floor of the shower stall doesn't look blatantly dirty, but it's old and cracked. I can just imagine the amount of bacteria lurking on it, ready to attack bare skin and cause a foot fungus. Thank goodness for my shower shoes.

Foot fungus is not an option.

I hang my toiletries and PJs on the only hook in the stall. Getting undressed is not easy to do while you're wearing shower shoes. I balance on one foot as I slip out of my dirty shorts, but unfortunately my ballet skills aren't translating to shower balance.

Like a movie in slow motion, my naked body slips on the cement.

I make a huge noise that comes out as "Whoooaaa!" but it really sounds like that big ape-looking guy from *Star Wars* that Mitch made me watch when we dated. He made me come over to his house one Saturday and watch all six episodes. That's over twelve hours of movies in one day, if you include the deleted scenes. Once, in the middle of making out during Episode 5, Mitch asked if I wanted to see his Wookie. I sat up and slapped him. I mean, we'd only been going out for a few weeks and the thought of his "thingie" being a short, hairy thing grossed me out.

Mitch said later, after putting ice on his cheek to reduce the swelling from the hand-shaped red mark of my slap, that he only wanted to show me his set of Wookie figurines. As *if*.

"You okay?" I hear Jessica's voice echo in the other stall.

Okay, so now that I slipped/fell, I'm on all fours on the floor. I guarantee that no matter how fast I get up, the five-second rule doesn't count. I've for sure got things that grow in petri dishes on my hands, knees, and butt.

I turn the water on, refusing to be bacteria-ridden for even one more second. I'm ready to wash off the dirt and dust and bacteria and stress from my first day as an IDF trainee.

I stick my hand in the water to test the temperature. It's cold.

I turn the crank in the opposite direction, then test again.

It's still cold.

Maybe it needs time to warm up. So I wait a minute, then test again.

Still cold.

Now I'm starting to shiver, because I'm naked and the temperature has definitely dropped at least twenty degrees from this afternoon.

"Three more minutes!" Ronit yells from the door.

I pull the curtain aside and stick my head out. "Ronit, I think there's something wrong with my shower. There's no hot water."

"There's no hot water in mine either," Jessica cries out from her stall. "Brrr!"

"None of us have hot water," one of the girls from New York says as she gathers up her stuff and exits the shower. Seriously, she took an entire shower in less than four minutes...how clean can she be?

Ronit chuckles and says with a big smile, "Welcome to the IDF! You have two minutes left!"

With that warning, I quickly dip into the cold water. Wet and freezing, I quickly lather my hair with shampoo and squirt liquid soap on my poofy sponge. My teeth chatter as I soap myself and quickly plunge under the sprinkling showerhead.

As I'm rinsing, Ronit yells out, "One minute!"

I have to admit, my bottles of shampoo and liquid soap are scattered at my feet. I'm not thinking about bacteria anymore. I'm thinking about my hair conditioner, and how crappy my hair is going to look if I don't put it on. On top of that, I think I just bit my tongue because of my chattering teeth.

Halfway through squirting conditioner on my hair, I hear Ronit give us a "thirty seconds!" warning.

Oh, crap.

I don't even have my conditioner spread, and already I have to rinse it off. Does Ronit know how much Aveda minty-smelling conditioner costs? Not that she would care, but still.

"Amy, come on," Jessica whispers to me. "You have, like, ten seconds. Are you done?"

I pull my dirty clothes off the hook to get to my PJs from behind them. Unfortunately, my PJs fall onto the wet ground because the hook is too small. Taking a deep breath and pulling on my yellow polka-dot pajama bottoms (now wet in spots) and matching yellow top, I grab everything and run out.

"Tomorrow you'll have to do ten pushups for each minute you're late," Ronit informs me.

While we walk back to our barracks, Jessica blows hot air on her hands. "I'm freezing."

My teeth are still chattering as I look down at my thin nightshirt. "I think I'm going to be permanently nippy." I can't help but notice, again, that I have the biggest boobs out of our entire unit by far. I got my blue eyes from my Israeli grandmother, my black curly hair from my father, and my huge saggy boobs from my mom. Okay, so they're not as saggy as my mom's are ... she's pregnant.

Did I mention that soon I'm not going to be an only child anymore? Yep, my mom and stepdad Marc *"with a c"* decided to have a baby. So now I'm going to have a brother or sister young enough to be my kid.

Back in the barracks, I open my suitcase and slip a University of Illinois sweatshirt over my wet, shivering head. Then I open my makeup case and do my nightly routine: take residue makeup off, put toner and moisturizer on, then spritz refresher spray for that extra misty-sparkle to make my skin look radiant (I know I sound like a commercial, but I did model once and my mom is in the advertising business).

After flat-ironing my hair, I pull out my favorite pillow from home. It's completely encased in a hot pink silk pillowcase. I set it on my bed. One of the New York girls, Victoria (aka Vic), is on my top bunk. Vic climbs up and the springs squeak as her weight presses down on the thin mattress.

I look up at the exposed springs. I hadn't noticed them before, but now I see why Jessica (who shall now be deemed the "manipulative traitor") wanted to switch bunks with me. The small springs keeping the mattress (and Vic) from falling on my face are attached with an S-type looking metal thingy. The problem is that almost every other spring is broken, missing, or super worn-out.

I'm not the claustrophobic type normally, but watching the mattress sink lower every time Vic moves makes me nervous.

I mean, seriously, what if Vic overstresses the *one* spring that's keeping all the rest from snapping off. It's like the game Jenga or that ice-breaking game. One wrong move and it's all over—SPLAT!

Out of the corner of my eye, I see Jess waving to get my attention. I narrow my eyes at my best friend. She puts her hand to her heart and mouths the word *sorry*, although she looks more amused than sorry. I think sometimes her brother Ben, aka *the demon from hell* (even though I'm Jewish and don't believe there's a hell), has rubbed off on her. One of his regular stunts is tossing chunks of *challah* bread across the Shabbat table with the purpose of getting one stuck in my cleavage. When he's successful, he grins and offers to take it out.

"Lights out in four minutes!" Ronit calls.

I wave to Miranda, who's on the bottom bunk two away from mine, across the aisle. I pull up my painfully thin blanket and try to get comfortable. It's not easy to relax with stretched-out springs squeaking overhead every time my bunkmate moves. I should watch all the food that goes into Vic's mouth during the next ten days. I can't risk her gaining weight while we're here, that's for sure … my life may depend on it.

Seriously, if the springs do give out in the middle of the night and she falls on me, will I suffocate and die? And if I do, will anyone care? Maybe I should sleep on my side, so if the springs collapse and the mattress and Vic fall on me, I might still have a little air pocket and live.

I'm definitely feeling sorry for myself tonight, but then I think of the Israeli soldiers who have to sleep on a bottom bunk staring up at missing and broken springs every night for years. I'm only here for a little over a week.

When Ronit flips off the lights, I turn on my side (partially because I like sleeping on my side) and think about Avi lying in his bunk.

Is he in pain from the pushups?

Is he lying on the top bunk, or bottom?

Is he thinking about me as much as I'm thinking about him?

When Avi stayed at my house back in January, he never wore a shirt to bed. I loved staring at his abs and biceps. I would kiss him good night and he'd flash me one of his rare smiles as he pulled me close (of course this was when my dad wasn't hawking us and ordering me back to my room).

I don't have my cell phone with me to listen to his old voicemail messages. He left them when we broke up during his visit and he was as desperate as I was to get back together. I know those messages by heart, and repeat them in my head…

> *Did I tell you your eyes remind me of blown glass? I can see your soul through those eyes, Amy. They get darker when you're trying to be sexy and they shine when you smile. And when you think you're in trouble you blink double the amount that you usually do. And when you're sad, the corners of your eyes turn down. I miss your eyes.*
>
> *I want to say something to you. Not because I want you to say it back, either.* (insert deep breath

here) *I… I love you. It's not that kind of condi-*
tional love… it's the kind that'll be around forever.
Even if you don't call. Even if you like Nathan or
any other guy. We can be friends. We can be more.
Just… call me back.

Did I mention when I first met you I was so
attracted to you it scared me? Me, scared. I still am
when I'm around you, because now I want you in
my life forever. How long is forever, Amy?"

I wish his arms were around me right now, assuring me that this is just another bump in the road of our rocky but passionate relationship.

I fall asleep, thinking of the day when Avi will hold me all night long without parental (or military) interference.

10

Lack of sleep has many, many negative consequences.

I'm dreaming that someone is turning on the lights and yelling in my ear.

"You have seven minutes to be dressed and outside! Bring your canteens!"

No, this isn't a dream. It's a nightmare. And I'm living it.

"I'm tired, Ronit. I just got to sleep," I hear Tori moan.

Her complaint is met by a "*Yala, zooz!*"

I hear some of the other girls talking, but instead of waking me up, the sound lulls me back to sleep.

"Amy, wake up!" Miranda says, shaking me like I'm the lulav branch during Sukkot.

"I'm up," I murmur.

"No, you're not. Come on! The guys from our unit are already outside."

I pull my pink silky pillow over my head. "I'm taking a mental health day."

"There are no mental health days in the military. Avi's there, too," she whispers in my ear.

I jump out of bed and give myself a nasty head rush. I strip off my PJs, strap on a bra, and get in my military uniform (which consists of an olive green button-down shirt and matching pants). I toss the matching floppy hat into my cubby because there's no way I'm wearing it, and slip on my new red high-tops. Opening my makeup case, I know I only have time for minimal application.

"What are you doing?" Tori asks with a stupid sneer on her face.

"What does it look like I'm doing? I'm putting on makeup."

Tori rolls her eyes. "Do you think you're going to a party?"

I sneer back, one of my famous sneers that beats hers hands-down. The only sneer that can rival mine is my cousin O'snot's.

I quickly apply eyeliner, mascara, and colored lip gloss while everyone scrambles around.

Once outside, with my canteen strapped on my shoulder like a very ugly purse, I get in formation while I watch Avi. It's still dark, but I can see him clearly in the lighted courtyard. He doesn't look tired; he doesn't look as if he's just woken up before God did. And today he's wearing a huge military vest with pockets, filled with ammunition or whatever military stuff he's supposed to carry. To top it off, he's got on a military backpack and his rifle. He looks as if he's about to go on some dangerous mission and is able, willing, and ready for war.

Nathan, on the other hand, looks horrible. He's got really bad bed-head, and is obviously super tired because his eyes are at half-mast.

Liron, with her ever-present big-ass rifle, asks Avi a question as she points to the papers on the clipboard she's carrying. He quickly glances at me, then nods to her.

I'm trying to concentrate on Ronit's lecture about time … something about time being important and how it could mean the difference between life and death in war. She says we have to move faster. But I'm not listening, because I'm too busy wondering what Liron and Avi were just talking about. Besides, someone needs to clue Ronit in that we're just civilian trainees on a "fun" summer program. The brochure didn't say anything about actually going into combat.

Sergeant B-S is mysteriously absent. I think he must be getting his beauty sleep. Avi, Nimrod, and three other Sayeret Tzefa trainees are in charge of our unit for this exercise. Ronit and Liron are coming along, too.

They make us stop by a big spigot coming out of the ground.

"Make a line and fill your canteens," Avi orders in a

loud Israeli accent. He stands in front of the spigot, supervising, as we wait our turn to fill our canteens.

When it's my turn, Avi puts his hand on the small of my back. I swear that electrons or protons, or whatever they taught us in biology class is in your body, zing up my spine. This boy, this man, this *soldier*...one minor touch from him reminds me of the time we were in my car on the beach back in Chicago. There were no parents, no friends, no military commanders around, no rules...it was just the two of us. My mind wanders back to that night...

> *"I want to forget how inexperienced you are," Avi groans as he leans back on the headrest of the car.*
>
> *"So teach me," I say. I bite my lower lip as I reach up and unbutton the top two buttons of my shirt, well aware Avi's eyes are now totally focused on my task as I move my hands lower and start unbuttoning the rest. My hands are shaking—I'm not sure if it's from the cold car or my trembling nerves.*
>
> *"Didn't you listen when your dad had the sex talk? Didn't he tell you boys only want one thing?"*
>
> *"Do you, Avi? Do you only want one thing?" I say as I open my shirt and reveal my bra beneath it.*
>
> *"I have to be honest and say my body's only thinking about one thing right now."*
>
> *"Take your shirt off," I order.*

As his hands reach for the hem of his shirt he says in a strained voice, "Your dad's gonna kill me." He lifts his shirt over his head and tosses it onto the driver's seat with his eyes never leaving me.

As he brushes the tips of his fingers across my abdomen, the tingles send wild sensations through my body. "Are you okay with this?" he asks, his face serious.

I nod and give him a small smile. "I'll let you know when I'm not."

As I lean down to press our bodies against each other, his hands reach around under my open shirt and pull me toward him. "Your body . . . so warm."

His hands are like a fire, consuming my body with his touch. I lean my head on his chest, hearing his heart beating the same erratic rhythm as my own while his hands move up and caress my hair, my bare back, and my breasts.

As I reclaim his lips, raw emotions and new wonderful feelings whirl in my consciousness. I'm fully aware I'm not ready to have sex, but I'm ready to experience more . . .

"You okay?" Avi asks me, bringing me back to the reality of my life called boot camp. I wish we were in my car right now instead of here.

"Uh, yeah. Are you?"

Avi wants to be a hardass in the IDF and not show

emotion. He once told me I'm the one person who makes him emotional, and that scares him.

I think of how I lured him to spend time alone with me yesterday. I guess deep down I knew if I begged him to go somewhere private with me he wouldn't refuse—even if it was against the rules. I have the power to make him forget the rules, and I abused that power.

Oh, no! I'm like Eve in the Garden of Eden, and he's poor Adam. Amy = The Dark Side.

My canteen is full, so I have to step aside. "Do you hate me?" I murmur.

He shakes his head and smiles. "No."

"I'm sorry you had to do pushups yesterday."

He examines his roughed-up palms. "I deserved it."

I feel a tension between us. I'm desperate for that tension to go away.

"Amy, I have to tell you something."

Good. I hope he says he loves me. I hope he says he's glad I'm here. I hope he says he wishes we were alone together. I gaze into his eyes and say in a hopeful voice, "What? What do you want to tell me?"

"Wear your hat."

"My hat?" Is he kidding me?

"Wear it. It's for your protection."

"I look dorky in hats, Avi. I'm not wearing it."

"You'll look worse with sunburn."

"Thanks for the tip," I say, kind of sarcastically, then head back into formation. I'm not wearing the hat, and

I'm sulking. I know I shouldn't expect Avi to say romantic stuff to me while we're here, but I want to hear those things coming out of his mouth nonetheless.

When everyone's canteen is full, we get fifteen minutes to scarf down breakfast, then we head out the gates of the army base in perfect formation. We march to Avi's *small-ya'mean-smalls* for a while. Every so often he orders all of us to drink from our canteens. It's no sparkling Perrier, and it's not cold, but it's wet and feels good going down my throat.

Avi and two other guys are standing in front of us, rifles cradled in their hands. The other Sayeret Tzefa trainees are flanking us on all sides.

You'd think I'd be freaked out with all the rifles and military precautions. But I'm not. I know the risks of being in Israel, and so do the Israelis. While they go on with their daily lives, refusing to give in to the fear of terrorism, they do what they can to protect themselves. I feel safe with these warriors protecting me.

We continue marching. This time Nimrod calls out the marching chant. The dawn chill disappears and the air grows warmer, a hint the sun will be up soon. The longer we march, the more the landscape looks like a barren desert. Mountains and rocks are our only scenery, and the uneven pebbly ground meets our shoes.

Some kids at school have asked me what's so special about Israel. It's not like there's a fun amusement park to go to or specific "wonders of the world" like the pyramids in Egypt. Israel is special just by being here—if you've never been to Israel, you can't fully "get it." You can tell you're in Israel because of the people. Israeli citizens are determined and strong. They're harsh, but have a heart. They refuse to let terrorism or fear disrupt their daily lives—maybe it's because of the Holocaust and maybe it's because they've lived in a war zone for so long. Whatever it is, their determination to live life to the fullest, without fear, is contagious.

The land of Israel mimics the citizens of its country. The harsh landscape of the Negev desert makes you wonder why people settled here, until you reach the historical sites and are awed by the rich history of the land. Where my cousins live, in the Golan Heights, you wonder why anyone would live so far from civilization until you step to the edge of the mountain—the Sea of Galilee shines at you and confirms your belief in God all over again.

I'm not feeling the mystical effect of Israel right now, though, because I haven't had enough sleep to appreciate the Jewish homeland. Just when I'm about to complain about rocks in my high-tops, we're ordered to stop and take another five-minute rest.

I'm talking to Jessica and Miranda when Nathan walks up to us. "I feel like Moses wandering in the desert for forty years," he says.

"Why do you think they brought us here?" Miranda asks as she wipes her sweaty face with her sleeve.

Jess shrugs. "Beats me. I'm hot and crabby. Amy, go ask Avi why we're here."

"No."

"Why not?" Nathan asks. "He's your *soulmate*, right? Isn't that what you called him last week when I asked why you were saving yourself for that big oaf?"

"Um, uh, I hate to break the bad news, but that big oaf is standing right behind you," Jess informs him.

Nathan looks at Miranda. "Tell me she's lying," he groans.

Miranda's answer is a rapid shake of her head.

Avi shoves a shovel the length of his arm at Nathan.

"What's this for, to dig my own grave?" Nathan asks as he takes the shovel out of Avi's grip.

"I'm not that lucky," Avi says. "Follow me."

Everyone else is assembling next to a soldier from Sayeret Tzefa. In all, there are five groups of eight people, each with a small shovel. Avi's team consists of me, Jessica, Miranda, Tori, Nathan, and three other American guys named David, Eli, and Ethan.

"This is a contest," Nimrod says. His group stands next to ours, and Avi is stoic as he watches Nimrod explain. "You have to dig a ditch two meters long and one hundred centimeters deep. The winning group gets a ride back to base camp."

Oh, we are SO winning this since Avi is on our team. I clap my hands excitedly and pat my boyfriend's back.

"Don't be too excited. Team leaders can't help."

Huh? Without his help, there's no way we can win. We've got Tori on our team, and after spending a day with her, I know she's going to be a pain in the butt. Nathan's got this testosterone fight going on with Avi so his focus isn't on the prize. We've got Miranda, but she's still panting and sweating from the hike. If pushed more, she might just pass out. David, Eli, and Ethan are all from big cities and are staring at the shovel as if it's a foreign object.

We're hopeless.

"Put your canteens down," Avi orders.

He's treating me just like everyone else. It bothers me. I want him to act like my boyfriend and let everyone know we're a couple. Yes, I'm aware it's selfish and immature, but at least I'm willing to admit it.

"Start digging!" Nimrod orders.

We all look to Avi for direction. He's standing with his arms crossed on his chest, watching us, not saying anything.

"He's obviously not going to help us," I inform my group. "You have the shovel, Nathan. Start digging."

Nathan picks a spot on the ground and starts digging. Dirt and rocks are flying in the air behind him as he quickly gets to work.

After ten minutes, he stops. "My fingers are starting to get numb." He hands the shovel to me. "Your turn."

I take the shovel and start where Nathan left off. I think I'm doing pretty well, although my team is totally annoying.

"Dig harder," Ethan urges.

"Faster!" David screams when I feel a fingernail break and stop digging for a fraction of a second to check it.

The problem is, we're not digging in the sand. We're digging up rocks that may have been here for hundreds, if not thousands, of years. Maybe our holy forefathers Abraham, Isaac, and Jacob walked on these rocks we're digging. It's not an easy task, and now the sun has come up and hits me in the face. I wish I had my sunglasses, because now I'm squinting. I'll be able to blame my premature wrinkles on this rock-digging experience.

I feel a tickle on the back of my hand. I need to scratch it, but don't want to stop digging because I want to (1) show Avi that I can be a good ditch-diggin' soldier and (2) I don't want to *small-ya'mean-small* back to the base. I really want a ride.

When the itching bugs me so much I can't ignore it, I hesitate and look down at my hand.

Oh! My! God!

There is a HUGE creepy black spider crawling on me. I throw down the shovel and shake my hand vigorously.

"AAAHHHHHH!" I scream and run, not able to stop the heebie jeebies. I keep shaking my hand just in case the creepy crawler is still on me.

What if it bites me?

What if it's poisonous?

What if it crawls up my sleeve?

What if it already laid creepy spider babies on me!

"What's wrong?" Jess cries out.

"Are you hurt?" Miranda yells over my screams in a concerned voice.

"Did something bite you?" Nathan calls.

I can't stop to explain, because I'm still jumping around and shaking like a madwoman.

I'm barely aware of Avi attempting to subdue me. I flail my arms and slap his hands away because I'm still worried the spider is on me.

But then Avi twirls me around so my back is against his and he wraps his arms around me so tight I can't move.

I'm breathing hard and I'm sweaty and smelly and totally freaked out from spiders and embarrassment because everyone is watching me.

Now I'm in Avi's arms, which are like a vice holding me still.

"Was it a crav?"

"No, not a crab," I gasp. Do crabs even live in the desert?

"I didn't say crab. *Ah'crav* ... a, uh ... " He's searching his brain for the English word so he can translate. "Scorpion?" he finally says.

"No."

"Are you hurt?" he asks. He's so calm I stop struggling against him.

"I don't know. It was ... " I choke out the word. "A spider."

"A *spider*?"

Everyone else laughs hysterically.

"I ... I think it was a black widow. It was really big! And hairy! And it was crawling on my SKIN!"

"Black widows aren't hairy," he says, but instead of making fun of me like everyone else, my boyfriend turns me around, takes my hands in his, and inspects them. "It's gone."

"What if it crawled up my shirt?" I say, squirming. I swear I feel little prickly legs on my back. It could be my imagination, like when you're talking about lice and you start scratching. But it really feels like spiders are crawling all over me.

"Don't panic."

I keep squirming. "I'm afraid it's still on me. Avi, help me. Please," I beg.

Without hesitation, he picks me up like I weigh close to nothing and calls out for Liron to follow us.

He hurries behind a large boulder. "Take your shirt off. Nobody can see you." He turns around, giving me privacy.

I unbutton the shirt as fast as I can while Liron stands next to Avi. Her back is to me, too. I think he called her over because he didn't want to have our entire unit see him take me somewhere alone. He doesn't want us to get in trouble again.

Liron is our chaperone.

I can't believe I need a chaperone when I'm with my boyfriend.

"Okay, it's off. I'm not going back out there in my bra." I mean, Avi's seen me with just a bra on, but not in public.

Avi holds out his hand, his back still to me. "Give it to me."

"My bra?"

He glances back at me, even though we both know one word from Liron to Sergeant B-S about him seeing me with no shirt will probably have him doing pushups again. "No. The shirt."

After I hand it to him, I watch him carefully inspect it from top to bottom. He turns it inside out, making sure it's free of creepy crawlers. He even opens the pockets and inspects those.

He tosses the shirt back to me. "There's nothing on it, or in it. Trust me."

"Thanks," I say. If there's anyone at the top of my trust list, it's Avi. Now that I'm calm, I can't confirm that the spider was hairy. And maybe it wasn't as big as I made it out to be.

Liron shakes her head. "If I didn't see it with my own two eyes, I wouldn't believe it."

"What can't you believe?" I ask her.

"Avi Gefen inspecting a shirt for a spider."

"Why?" My boyfriend is my hero; why shouldn't he help me?

Liron chuckles. "Avi tells everyone else in Sayeret Tzefa to suck it up, whether they're tired, bleeding, or throwing up from exhaustion. But with you ... and a little spider ... " She shakes her head. "I don't get it."

After I have the shirt back on, they both turn around

to face me. Avi points to me as he talks to Liron. "You saw her—she was freaking out."

"And you came to her rescue. She's ruining your reputation."

"She's my girlfriend," Avi says defensively. "What would you want me to do?"

"Treat her like a soldier, like you treat the rest of us. She didn't sign up to be rescued, she signed up to be a trainee."

"This isn't about Amy. It's about us."

Wait. One. Second. Did he just say "us" as in Avi and Liron "us" ... not Amy and Avi "us"?

"Oh, shit." Avi rubs his temples as he squeezes his eyes shut. "I didn't mean to say that in English."

Fear, deep and strong, slices through my body. I'm afraid to ask, but can't stop myself more than I can stop myself from breathing.

"What are you saying, Avi? Are you two, like, a couple or something?"

11

---

milk + meat = not kosher

my boyfriend + kissing another girl = not kosher

I turn to Liron for answers.

"Avi, tell her," Liron says.

"Yeah. Tell me." When he hesitates, my entire body goes numb. "It doesn't matter, anyway, because Nathan and I have been dating since February, after you left. I wanted to tell you, but I didn't want to upset you."

Phew. I can't believe I got the lie out without choking.

Crunching stones alerts us that someone is about to join us. It's Nimrod. He looks at Liron, then Avi, then me. "*Hakol Beseder*—everything okay? No more spiders?"

"No spiders," I say. "And everything is just hunky-dory. Right, Avi?"

I lied to Liron and Avi because I didn't know what else

to do. I'm in total shock. Was everything Avi told me back in Chicago about how much he loves me a complete lie? Were all those letters he wrote me lies, too? He knows I have trust issues because my parents never married and I didn't even have a relationship with my father until last year.

No wonder Avi doesn't want me here. He wants to be free to have his relationship with Liron on base and then have me, his American girlfriend, on the side.

Ugh, the thought of it makes me sick.

I storm back to my group, leaving Nimrod with the lovebirds. Okay, Avi and Liron don't look or act like lovebirds, but he's obviously dating her behind my back. And I'm obviously the idiot girlfriend thinking it was worth it to spend time at a military boot camp to see my boyfriend.

Now I'm stuck. I would quit, but I begged my dad to sign me up and there's no turning back now. If I leave with my tail between my legs, I can just imagine what my dad will say. *I told you you're too young to have a serious relationship with Avi. I told you the program wouldn't be easy, and you couldn't handle military life. Next time listen to your father.*

I glare at anyone laughing at me. Every comment, every snicker, is like nails dragging down a chalkboard, making me cringe.

Jess runs up to me. "Amy, are you okay?"

"I'm fine," I snap back, which earns me a weird look from my best friend.

"Did you get bitten?" Miranda asks me.

"No. I don't want to talk about it."

Our team hasn't finished digging the hole yet, although all the other teams have. Nimrod's team is giving themselves high fives, so I assume they're the winners of the challenge.

Liron orders her team into formation without looking my way.

Avi peers down into our pathetic, three-inch-deep hole.

"We lost," Nathan tells him. "Which isn't a big surprise considering we had one less person and no team leader after you guys disappeared."

"We're not going back until our ditch is finished," Avi informs us. "No giving up."

Like he did with our relationship?

Since Avi left Chicago, I haven't thought of anyone else. I haven't been remotely interested in another guy because I know he's The One. He said we were going to be together forever, that he wanted to marry me one day. I believed him, which makes me the dummy.

Listen, I know I have to finish high school, go to college, and get a job. But I also thought my future included Avi, too.

A big army truck comes into sight, kicking up desert dust in its wake. Nimrod and his team hop on and, within a minute, are out of sight.

My team members are still shoveling, per Avi's orders. I'm purposely ignoring anyone with a name that starts with an *A*, has an *I* at the end, and a *V* in the middle. I can feel his eyes boring into my back like Superman's X-ray vision. But my boyfriend isn't Superman, at least not anymore.

And now, to save face, I have to pretend Nathan and I are in love. I'm not sure Nathan will go for the charade. Dare I tell him? He's afraid enough of Avi as it is.

Avi tells the rest of the teams to file out and head back to base while we finish digging. Tori is shoveling, although she's not going fast and I think we might be here for a few days. We're all so hot and sweaty I wonder if skin can actually melt off of our bones.

"Amy..." I hear Avi's voice from behind me.

"Is someone talking to me?" I ask Jess. "Because all I hear is hot air." I tap on my ears with my palms, pretending to clear my ear canals.

Miranda taps me on the shoulder and nudges me to turn around. "Avi's right behind you, Amy. Maybe you really did get bit by that spider and it affected your hearing."

Thanks, Miranda. *Not*. The girl is not too quick on social cues, that's for sure. I love Miranda to death (okay, not to *death*... that's a bit over the top), but she can definitely use lessons in how to not take everything so literally.

I turn to Avi with a cool smile on my face. "Did you want something, O Unfaithful One?"

"Don't say that."

"Why not? It's true, isn't it?"

"You walked away before I could explain, Amy."

"So explain now."

"Not with an audience."

"We have no choice, Avi, do we?" I focus on kicking a large rock. "Did you sleep with her?"

All conversations immediately stop. Everyone waits for Avi to answer. I think the air even stops moving (although I can't say that's a big feat because there wasn't a breeze to begin with).

"No, I didn't sleep with her—"

"Did you kiss her?"

"Can we not do this *now*?"

"No, we're gonna do this right here, right now. Did you kiss her?"

"Yes."

"I can't believe you!" I attempt to shove him away from me, but the guy is like a solid rock of muscle. He grips my wrists and holds them away.

"You kissed Nathan, remember?" he says, his eyes blazing. "And now you say you're dating him. Is that true, Amy?"

"No, it's not!" Nathan calls out.

I narrow my eyes at Nathan. "There's no need to keep us a secret anymore, Nathan. I told Avi about us."

"But—"

Nathan's words are cut short when Jess pushes him into our team's ditch and he falls right onto Tori.

"Where's your honor and integrity, Avi?" I throw back the words he said to me back in January when he found out I'd kissed Nathan.

"You said we shouldn't be exclusive. You said it wasn't realistic to think we wouldn't be attracted to other people."

The thought of him being attracted to Liron is too

much for me to deal with. "I was just *saying* that," I yell at him. "I didn't want you to actually *do* it."

He lets go of my wrists as if they're on fire and he's about to get burned. "Next time, say what you mean."

"Like you meant it when you said you wanted to marry me one day? It was all lies, Avi."

"You know that's not true."

"Cheating boyfriends become cheating husbands."

"I didn't chea—" Avi runs his hand over his grown-out buzz cut. "Just let me know. Are we breaking up?"

"That depends. Did you kiss Liron just once?"

"No."

"Twice?"

"No."

"Three times?"

"Amy…"

"Answer me, Avi. Three times?"

"I didn't count."

"Maybe you should have. What did you think, that you could just fast for Yom Kippur come September, repent it one day, and God would wipe your sinning slate clean? What, you think God has only one book? I bet he's got *lots* of books, Avi, just filled with names of sinners. Because while God may inscribe you in the Book of Life for another year, he's probably also inscribing you in the Book of Cheaters."

His eyes get darker when he's angry. They're definitely dark now. "Whatever, Amy. I can't talk to you when you're being irrational. If God's got a Book of Irrational People, *you're* at the top of the list." He whips off his backpack and picks up our team shovel from the ground. "Get out," he orders Tori and Nathan, who immediately scramble out of the ditch.

Avi sheds his military vest. We all watch in awe as Avi finishes digging in less than three minutes.

When he's done, we get back in formation and start marching back to base. After a half hour, he gives us a five-minute break and orders us to drink from our canteens. He does this every half hour. When we reach the base, he orders us to drink what's left in our canteen.

I'm too angry to drink.

He steps in front of me. I can feel the heat of the mid-morning sun, but I can also feel the heat of Avi's gaze on me. "Amy, finish the water."

"Maybe I already did."

"I might be just a sheep farmer to you back at the *moshav*, but here I outrank you whether you like it or not. Drink it all, or you'll dump whatever's left in the canteen on your head."

A bee decides to hover between us. I hate bees almost as much as spiders.

"There's a bee about to sting us," I say, hoping to make him flinch, or at least get a reaction to remind me he's human.

No such luck.

"Drink or dump," he orders.

I could drink what's left in my canteen, but my ego is

fragile and rebellious. I'm holding on to the little control I have left.

"Yes, sir!" I say sarcastically, then salute my now ex-boyfriend.

I slowly lift my canteen over my head. Avi is watching intently. I'm pretty sure the odds are 80 percent he'll stop me before a drop of liquid lands on my head, 20 percent he'll let me go through with the water-dumping. He has always come to my rescue in the past. This time, though, he's the one I need rescuing from.

When my canteen is directly over my head, I realize there's a 100 percent chance he won't stop me.

Pouring water on myself means that my straightened hair will end up a random, curly mess. I can't do it.

"Do it."

I clench my teeth and lift my chin in defiance. "No."

Avi grabs my canteen, lifts it over my head, and turns it upside down. Water rushes down my scalp, making the hairs on the back of my neck stick straight up. It drips onto my neck and runs down my back. Little rivers run down my face. I must look ridiculous, and it's all Avi's fault.

"You cooled off yet?" Avi asks.

"Not by a long shot."

He shoves the empty canteen in my hand, then eyes the rest of the team. "When you're finished, hold your canteen above your head and turn it upside down."

A few people quickly drink what's left in their canteen, making sure not to leave a drop. I'm the only one with a mid-morning sprinkle.

I'm trying not to pay attention to Avi, but I can't help it. Against my better judgment, I focus on his lips. They're full and soft to the touch—I know because I've felt them with my fingers and my own lips.

Ugh. I cannot believe Liron had her lips against his. I shudder just thinking about it.

When Avi dismisses us to our *bittan* for cleanup time, I corner Nathan in the courtyard in front of the girls' barracks. I wrap my arms around his neck and kiss him lightly on the lips. "Please play along while Avi's watching," I whisper in his ear.

"You're the devil," he says. "Stay away from me while your boyfriend's around."

"He's not my boyfriend," I assure him as I shoo away another hovering bee. "Not anymore, at least."

"Neither am I, so stop telling everyone I am. I'm trying to get into Tori's pants, you know."

"Eww. Why?"

"She's cute, she's a dancer ... I even hear she's double-jointed. I've never been with a double-jointed girl before."

"You're sick, and totally acting like Kyle, the biggest perv in school."

"I'm a *guy*, Amy. What do you expect?"

Up until a few weeks ago, Nathan was still obsessed with his ex-girlfriend Bicky. Not Becky ... Bicky. She's a total druggie and has made Nathan's life miserable, which is the main reason he came on the *Sababa* trip. He has to get over Bicky, but replacing one bitch with another is definitely not the answer.

"Just smile and pretend you love me."

He smiles, puts his arm around my shoulders, and leads me to the barracks. "I *do* love you, Amy. As a friend. And as a friend I'm going to tell you that I'd like to keep my ball sacs intact and not piss off your boyfriend or ex-boyfriend or whatever he is. He's got a gun bigger than my entire arm. And isn't that thing attached to the bottom of it a grenade launcher? Geez, Amy, even his gun is pimped."

I spill the beans to Nathan softly, as if nobody else knows yet. "He's been fooling around with Liron. He's probably dating her for all I know."

"I know. Our entire team got the rundown before he finished our ditch, remember?"

"Don't you feel sorry for me?"

"Amy, didn't you tell me during your conversion class that God gives us challenges to test how strong we are? Maybe this is your test." Now two bees are hovering around us. Nathan shoos them away. "Were bees one of the ten plagues back in Moses' time?"

"Nope."

"Well, God is obviously sending them as the eleventh plague. We had a bunch buzzing around our bunks yesterday. It's a miracle we haven't gotten stung."

The talk of plagues and getting stung makes me look for Avi. He's talking to a guy from Sayeret Tzefa, and looks murderous as he stares down Nathan and me. He tries to walk over to us, but the guy he's with pulls him back.

Nathan taps my shoulder. "Talk to him and find out what the deal is, Amy. 'Cause I'm not gonna act like your boyfriend just so you can save face. That's a cop-out, and the Amy Nelson-Barak I know isn't a coward or a cop-out."

"You sound like Rabbi Glassman," I tell him.

Nathan smiles wide, proud to be put in the same category as my awesome rabbi who sponsored my conversion to Judaism. He stands tall and proud, as if he's Abraham Lincoln addressing the United States Senate (without the top hat, of course). "Yes, well I'm smart beyond my seventeen years."

"Yeah, right. You just said you wanted to date Tori because she was double-jointed. You sounded like an idiot then. Don't push that 'smart beyond my seventeen years' crap."

"Yo, Nate, we gotta do cleanup!" Brandon, another guy on the *Sababa* trip, calls out.

Nathan chucks me under the chin. "I gotta go, Amy. While I probably just signed my death warrant by talking to you for so long, I have to go before Susu starts his inspection."

"Girls' inspection in fifteen minutes!" Ronit calls out. "Nathan, you better not drag your feet. You should have been at the guys' barracks five minutes ago!"

Nathan jogs off, his sandy blond, bed-head hair bouncing with each step and his shirt sticking to his back from the heat of the Israeli sun.

12

Bees are God's little reminder not to get too comfortable in life; something or someone is going to come out and sting you when you least expect it.

I walk into the girls' barracks (which is now a sauna because the stifling air doesn't move in here). I'm surprised my bed is already made, with perfectly tight hospital corners. Even my wool blanket is folded neatly at the foot.

Vic, who just finished making her bunk above me, clues me in. "Jessica did it."

When I turn around, my best friend gives me a big hug. I haven't told her what's up with Avi, but she obviously guessed from the conversation we had back at our ditch.

"So I guess that Avi guy isn't your boyfriend anymore, huh?" Tori says. "That's so ... sad. Are you okay?"

I'm holding it together by a thin thread, lucky to have Jess beside me for support in the face of Tori's fake concern. I don't believe for a minute that she cares about me and Avi. In fact, I catch a glimmer of triumph in her eyes. I wish a bee was around to sting her in the butt. I know that's rude, and Rabbi Glassman would say that wishing someone harm isn't being a righteous Jew. I can't help it.

Girls my age either love me or hate me, and I have no clue why it's so cut-and-dried. Jess says it's because I come across as confident, and even if I have insecurities I cover them up at all costs. So when the haters see a glimpse into my misery, they're all over it.

"It's not a big deal," I tell Tori as I kneel next to my bed and pull my flat iron out. "You can find someone else to worry about 'cause you're wasting your pity on me."

I plug it in (with the 220 voltage converter attached), thankful for (1) the lone outlet in the room and (2) that my trusty flat iron heats up in thirty seconds.

My hair is already dry from the mid-morning heat. I sit on the floor next to the outlet with my travel mirror and brush in hand, ready to make the curls disappear. Balancing the mirror between my knees, I clamp the flat iron and get to work on the frizzy, curly pieces.

"I can't believe you're doing your hair when we're supposed to be cleaning," one of the New York girls says.

Looking up, I explain. "I can't have half my hair curly and half straight. That would look stupid."

"So put it up in a ponytail, like I do. Then it would be out of your face and nobody would notice any imperfections."

"Great idea, but I don't look good with my hair in a ponytail. Right, Miranda?"

Miranda grunts an unintelligible answer. What's up with that? Is happy-go-lucky Miranda actually upset about something? Maybe she's hungry.

"Why do you have to look good all the time?" New York Girl asks.

That's a really tough question. I thought about it once. The thing about my life is that I've never had control over it. I was ... how can I put it nicely ... I was *a mistake*. My mom and dad met in college, got together one night, and oops! My mom was pregnant.

As much as I prayed for them to get married, they never did. It probably shouldn't have affected me as much as it has, but you never know what's going to be the "thing" in your life that defines you (or the thing you should talk to a therapist about at length). I didn't even have a relationship with my dad until a year ago, when he took me to Israel for the first time.

My looks ... my image ... I guess that's the only thing I can control. God knows I haven't been able to control the people in my family. And today just proved that I can't control my boyfriend. Yes, I admit I have control issues.

The New York girl has her hair in such a tight ponytail her eyes look like they're being pinned back. And she actually bought black military steel-toed boots for this trip. The closest thing I have to that are my cherry red high-tops.

She is still waiting patiently for an answer. I should

tell her the truth. But I don't, because little white lies are in that gray area of life I live in. Even if the military doesn't have any gray areas, I still do.

I tell a little white lie. "I want to look good to impress Nathan."

"The blond guy who played the guitar on the bus ride to the base?"

I point excitedly at my nose, as if I'm playing charades. "That's the one!"

"But rumors are going around that you're dating that Israeli commando guy who was your team leader today."

I go back to straightening my hair. "We dated a little, but it was casual."

Now that's *not* a little white lie. That's a big, honkin' lie. My relationship with Avi isn't casual at all!

I used to imagine our wedding. We'd get married on the *moshav* our families live on in the Golan Heights (I'd make sure it was far from the farm animals, so the poop stench wouldn't drive guests away). I'd wear a white, flowing wedding gown and Avi would be in a casual, light-colored suit. We wouldn't be able to take our eyes off each other as the rabbi performed the ceremony, and I'd circle him seven times in the traditional Jewish way. Our love would last forever and ever; we'd share our deepest darkest thoughts, and nothing could break the bond between us.

Yes, it's totally corny. But that's my fantasy.

I even had our kids' names picked out. We'd have four kids and none would be a mistake like I was. We'd have two boys and two girls, of course—remember, this is still my fantasy—and they would be named Micha (after Avi's brother who died, because Jewish people don't name their kids after living people, only dead people, which is weird to me, but whatever), Golan (where Avi was born), Maya (which means "water" and that's something you can't live without), and Abigail (which means "leader of joy"; I didn't grow up with joy and want our children to grow up with it).

Of course, now, my fantasy is totally ruined.

As I'm doing my hair, a bee starts buzzing in my ear and I seriously almost burn myself with my flat iron.

"Go away!" I tell the bee, as if it speaks English and can understand me. It won't leave me and my hair alone. It's as if the nasty little buzzer wants to build a nest in my hair.

No buzzing insect is getting near my hair if I have anything to say about it. "Go away!" I tell it again, swatting at it with my flat iron, hoping to scare it away. No such luck. I'm not thinking, just relying on a self-protective instinct, and I clamp the hot ceramic plates together when the bee gets too close. Eww! I've trapped the bee inside my flat iron.

The good news: the bee will never bother me again. The little buzzer, shall we say, is toast.

The very bad news: I have hot bee guts stuck on my hot flat-iron plates. Yuck! It even smells like burnt bee. I unplug the flat iron so the plates will cool off.

Tori scrunches her face up after seeing the corpse stuck to my flat-iron plates. "That's not very *green* of you, Amy."

"Umm ... for your information, being green means helping the environment." According to my "green" standards, I just saved the other animals from getting stung, thus helping the environment.

"Bees are *part* of the environment, Amy," Tori says with a snotty attitude. "These are just worker bees anyway. Worker bees don't sting."

They don't? I thought *all* bees sting. But Tori sounds really convincing, as if she's a bee expert, like she knows for a fact that these bees are harmless. I feel stupid that I don't know that little fact. I look at my flat iron again, totally grossed out, knowing that I'll have to scrape the bee guts off the thing once it cools off.

And I'm still stuck with my half-curly/half-straight hair.

If anything goes right on this trip, it'll be a miracle. I'm praying for it, because if miracles are going to happen I'd think God would want to start in the Holy Land. Right?

Ronit walks in the room for her inspection and I gather up my stuff and head to my bunk. After shoving everything into my suitcase, and placing the hot flat iron in between the towels in my cubby, I stand in front of my bunk at attention like everyone else.

Ronit, with her hands behind her back, walks up to each bed, nodding or shaking her head. She gives little comments to each of us on how we can improve. She even orders one of the girls to re-make her bed. Afterward, when she has nodded to all the beds (which I guess is the equivalent of giving it her kosher blessing), we head to the courtyard to once again get in formation.

"Amy, step out of formation. It's your turn to guard the *bittan*." She points to a gray metal folding chair in front of our barracks.

I step out of formation. The hot sun beats down on the chair, the one I'm supposed to sit on to guard our valuables. Seriously, who'd be dumb enough to steal stuff on an army base?

I swear there's no shade in this place so we're at the mercy of the blistering sun. I'm so hot that if I had SPF 50 on I'd be tempted to put on my bikini and lay out. How do the Israeli soldiers deal with living here in this heat, forced to wear long sleeves and long pants?

As my unit marches to lunch, I place the chair in the open doorway, out of the sun, thinking about Israeli teens and their mandatory military service. The Israeli teens don't seem to resent being soldiers. I think for some weird reason they look forward to putting on uniforms every day.

Fifteen minutes later, a soldier I've never seen before walks up to me holding a cafeteria tray with food on it. He's medium height with a round face and a friendly smile. Right about now a friendly smile is definitely welcome.

"*Shalom*," I say when he comes closer.

"You can speak English with me. I'm American, born and raised in Colorado. My name's Noah. I already know you're Amy —from Chicago."

Wait. Noah is American? But I thought he was a full-fledged soldier. He's dressed in a full IDF uniform with his last name in Hebrew on the front of his shirt. He also has a badge hanging off his shoulder with the logo of a military unit on one side and his rank on the other. None of the Americans on our *Sababa* trip have their last names sewn on their shirts, let alone a unit badge. Our shirts are totally blank. But he's not on our trip.

The guy is a poser; what's up with that? "I'm sure the soldier whose shirt you're wearing is looking for it."

The guy looks down at the Hebrew on the shirt. "This *is* my shirt." His smile broadens. "Phew. You had me worried there for a second."

"How'd you get them to put your name on it?" I notice he also has his own army boots, just like Avi's. Maybe he won a ditch-digging contest and the prize was his own personalized IDF uniform. "And how'd you get someone to give you their unit badge?"

"They kinda gave me the shirt and badge, along with the boots and inoculations when I enlisted."

"What do you mean by 'enlisted'?"

"I'm an Israeli soldier."

Before he'd opened his mouth and spoken perfect English without an accent, I'd assumed he was an Israeli soldier. He looks like one, and now I notice his rifle, but … "But you're American."

"I'm also Jewish. I came here after high school and volunteered for the IDF. I felt a connection to Israel and wanted to do my part to help my fellow Jews."

Gosh, that's admirable. Before now, I never heard of a Jewish American just coming over here and enlisting in the Israeli military. On purpose.

"Do you know Hebrew?" I ask, getting more curious.

"I know a lot more Hebrew now than when I first came here a year ago. You learn pretty quick when you have to." He hands me the tray of food. "Here, eat. Before it gets cold."

The food on the tray consists of a glass of water (with no ice), chicken (dark-meat legs, once again), mushrooms, and rice. Two bees have decided to hover around my food, which is totally annoying. But now that Tori told me worker bees don't sting, I'm not afraid like I was before.

"Thanks. I'm starving." I'm too hungry to care that I'll be eating greasy dark meat instead of white breast meat. I chew whatever's attached to the chicken bone as if it's my last meal on earth.

Noah sits against the door jamb and watches me eat.

"I thought IDF guys and *Sababa* teens can't be together alone."

"We're not alone," Noah says, pointing to the guard sitting at the entrance to the barracks across the courtyard.

"I'm the official guard," I tell him as I take a drink of warm water to wash down the food. "If you want to steal stuff, my job is to stop you. Although you have a gun and I don't, so feel free to pilfer whatever you want."

"I'm not here to steal stuff." Noah looks embarrassed as he places his rifle over his knees. "Gefen told me to come talk to you."

As I hear my boyfriend's last name, I almost choke on the slippery piece of dark meat or gristle or fat or skin or whatever greasy thing I'm trying to swallow. "Gefen who?"

"Avi Gefen."

"Oh, him." I say, as if Avi isn't on my mind 24/7. "What did he want you to talk to me about?"

"He kinda wanted me to give you a message."

"And he couldn't do that himself because … ?"

"Um, yeah. I think he said it had something to do with being afraid you'd break up with him before you hear him out. And maybe you'll listen to what he wants to tell you if it comes from someone else." Noah puts his hand up when I try to respond. "But don't quote me verbatim on that. I may have gotten a few words mixed up in the translation."

I point my half-eaten chicken leg at Noah. "You go tell Avi that we've already broken up, that I'm dating Nathan, and that if he's got something to say to me, be man enough to say it to my face. I don't want to hear things second-hand from a middleman."

"He doesn't believe you're dating whoever this guy Nathan is."

"Is he kidding? Nathan and I are … " I pick up the other uneaten chicken leg and hold it next to my half-eaten one. "Nathan and I are like this. Two chicken legs in a pod."

"Chickens don't come in a pod. Peas do."

"I don't see any peas around here, so I'm improvising. Work with me, Noah." This round-faced American-Israeli soldier would be a perfect match for Miranda. They're kind of the same person, but of the opposite sex.

Noah shrugs. "So you don't want me to relay his message?"

I shake my head.

He sighs. "Well, I hope you guys work it out at some point. Seeing Gefen upset isn't fun, especially during Krav Maga training."

I know a little Krav Maga—the official self defense of the Israeli military—because my dad was a commando when he was in the IDF. A few months ago he decided I was old enough to learn some of the contact combat basics. Essentially, it's to kick the person's ass (or groin, as my dad taught me) until your target is no longer a threat. If you can't get out of a bad situation, you strike hard, strike fast, and know the vulnerable places on your opponent's body.

My dad thought I would suck at it, but I actually did so well that after my first lesson he bought protective training pads. We've made training a weekly event. Krav Maga Night is my dad giving me new techniques on how to kick his ass, which I have to say is more therapeutic than a fifty-minute session with a social worker.

Seriously, what other teenager is lucky enough to say they're encouraged by their dad to punch, kick, and maim him every Wednesday? Although, given that my dad was a commando, he's specially trained to kick some ass himself.

Now that I live with my dad, we've worked out most

of our issues around him not being a permanent fixture in my life growing up. But he's still uncomfortable having a teen daughter when it comes to parental discussions about dating, sex, and drugs. The drug discussions (I'm using the word "discussion" loosely) go like this:

> *My dad: Amy, if you ever take illegal drugs I'll kill the person who gave them to you and then I'll kill you. Got it?*
> *Me: Loud and clear.*

The most recent sex talk (this time I'm using the word "talk" loosely) went along these lines:

> *My dad: Don't have sex until you're married.*
> *Me: What if I do?*
> *My dad: I'll practice Krav Maga on the guy. Without protective padding.*

I didn't mention then that my boyfriend is quickly becoming a Krav Maga legend in his own right on the base.

My dad is awful when it comes to talking about girly issues, as if he doesn't have a single ounce of estrogen in his body. But get him to talk about Krav Maga, or Israeli guy stuff like soccer or basketball, and his eyes light up.

"Thanks for the food!" I call out to Noah as he walks away, leaving me with my chicken bones, my folding chair, and thoughts of Avi—but not his message.

His answer is a wave and another smile.

Just when I finish lunch, I hear Ronit's *small-ya'mean-small* chant getting closer and closer.

"Amy, bring your tray to the eating area," Ronit says. "Miranda, go with her. Vic, you're in charge of guarding the *bittan* now."

I pick up the tray and start walking to the kitchen. Miranda walks with me...although she's actually a few paces behind. I have the feeling she's doing that on purpose.

"You okay?" I ask, glancing back at her.

She shrugs. "Sure."

"Because you're acting like something's wrong. Want to talk about it?"

"Nope."

Could it be that the Israeli army has broken Miranda's sweet-tempered spirit? I'm always crabby, but I thought I could count on Miranda to smile no matter what sucky situation she's in. I glance back again. The girl is definitely not smiling.

Maybe she's constipated. Seriously, talk to a group of teen girls in private and I guarantee they've all got pooping issues. Considering the lack of a decent toilet in this place, I wouldn't blame her.

But what if Miranda isn't constipated? What if she's upset with me? While I couldn't care less if Tori hates me, I do care if somehow I've caused this alienation between me and Miranda.

I wish Jess was ordered to accompany me, too. She'd know what to say to Miranda to make everything okay again.

As we walk into the cafeteria and I scrape the leftover food off my plate and into the big garbage bins, I realize Miranda isn't behind me anymore. She's waiting by the doorway with a pissy look on her face. I place the tray on the moving belt.

"Why aren't you smiling?" I ask her as we head back into the scorching Israeli death-heat.

"Because I don't feel like it. Why do you care, anyway? You hardly ever smile."

"Yeah, because I count on you doing it for me."

Miranda stops and puts her hands on her hips. "Amy, that doesn't even make sense."

"Neither does your pissy attitude. It reminds me of *me* and, to be honest, I wouldn't be able to stand a friend like me for very long."

"Are you saying I shouldn't be friends with you anymore?" She starts walking away, so I jog to catch up with her.

"When you smile, the world smiles with you, you know," I tell her.

I think she's about to laugh, but she doesn't. She starts walking faster. "You got that off of a greeting card or something."

"Well, if I was back home I'd run to Walgreens and get you a real card."

"What would you write in it?" she asks, challenging me to come up with something on the fly.

"I'd write…I'd write… *Don't be upset, Miranda. If I did anything to upset you, please forgive me. I know I'm not always a good friend to you. But if you share with me, I can try and fix it. Your friendship is really important to me, which says a lot about you because I can't stand most people. Being friends with you makes me a better person. So please don't give up on me. Love, Amy. P.S. When Nathan buys me another white chocolate Kit Kat, I'll give the entire thing to you."*

I have to give myself kudos. That was a damn good speech if I do say so myself. Any moment now sweet, shy-at-times/bubbly-at-times Miranda will turn back to her old self again. I stop and give her a look that says I know she's about to cave and envelop me in one of her big, embarrassing bear hugs. This time, I'm actually looking forward to it.

"I'll think about it," she says, then tosses her hair to the side and leaves me standing alone as she walks inside the barracks. No smile. No forgiveness. No bear hug.

Whoa. I just got a dose of Miranda the Diva dissing me.

13

---

*There's a point in time when even the strongest person
cracks under pressure.*

The next morning our unit marches across the large courtyard and doesn't stop until we get to what's obviously an
obstacle course. There's no doubt in my mind that this
will be a challenge for me.

"We'll be testing your strength and stamina," Sergeant
B-S says to us. "This course should be completed in less
than three minutes."

I tell myself not to look over at Avi, but as usual I
have a serious lack of self-control. My gaze wanders to
him and I find him looking straight at me. So now our
eyes are locked. My insides are melting, but I'm still angry
and hurt. Even though it's scorching hot outside and I can

feel the sweat running down my back and in between my boobs, a chill runs down my spine.

Sergeant B-S orders Nimrod and Avi to stand at the start of the obstacle course. Both get ready to race. When the sergeant blows his whistle, they take off faster than Mutt when he spots a new dog at the dog park.

I watch Avi whiz through the course as if he's been doing this his entire life. I can't help but admire the muscles that bulge from his arms as he jumps to the monkey bars and grabs the first bar, then skips two bars at a time until he's done. Then he crosses the balance beam.

When he gets to the high rope, he uses his thigh muscles and arms to pull himself to the top, rings the bell, then grabs a handle that brings him down to the ground. Nimrod is right behind him. At the half wall they're neck and neck.

I'm holding my breath, wondering who will win. They reach the part of the course where you duck low under a set of entwined ropes. Avi gains a little ground as he slithers on the ground, not hesitating one iota.

In the end, Avi is the one who crosses the line first. Nimrod is close behind him. Both are breathing heavily as Sergeant B-S tells us that Avi clocked in at thirty-eight seconds and Nimrod at forty-one.

Liron and Ronit line up next. When Sergeant B-S signals them to go, Liron blows Ronit away as she effortlessly does each obstacle. Ugh, no wonder Avi is attracted to her; not only is she pretty, but she can scale walls and shimmy up ropes. It's probably more impressive than being double-jointed. Liron clocks in at one minute one second while Ronit lags behind, finishing at one minute thirty seconds.

"Get in the same groups you were in yesterday," Sergeant B-S calls out.

I try to act cool as I walk over to Avi. Unfortunately, I'm not paying attention and trip over something or someone. Oops, it's Tori...I've stepped on the back of her foot again and her shoe came off.

"Ouch!" Tori yells out. "That's the second time you've done that, you spaz."

"Well maybe if you walked faster I wouldn't step on you."

Nathan grabs my shoulders. "Stop getting in fights with Tori," he says as he steers me away from her.

"She's rude."

"She's hot."

"So am I," I say as I wipe away another sweat drop that's falling down my forehead.

"I didn't mean hot as in sweaty. I mean hot as in—"

"I know what you meant," I say, cutting him off. Seriously, ever since Nathan finally stopped being obsessed with Bicky, he's been acting like a *Bachelor* reality show contestant. Since our third kiss and his breakup, he's gone out with more girls than I can count on two hands. And it doesn't help that he's been lead singer for Lickity Split, because lately he's been taking his groupies backstage and making out with them. He hasn't gone out with anyone twice yet. It's like he wants to make sure he doesn't get involved so there's no repeat of what he went through with Bicky. I wonder why the change in tactic since he met Tori.

I grab Nathan's hand while we wait for our other team members to assemble. Nathan pulls his hand loose, but I know Avi's watching so I grab his hand again and squeeze my nails into his skin as a warning not to snatch it back.

Avi growls, "Wait here" and walks away to talk to Liron and some of the other Israeli team leaders.

"You're getting me in trouble with Avi," Nathan says through gritted teeth and a fake smile which makes him look like a marionette on Prozac.

"Do you remember when you had me fake-kiss you in front of your ex-bimbo Bicky, to let her know it was over between you guys?"

"Yeah. I seem to remember you biting me."

"Nathan, that was because your tongue crept into my mouth."

"I was making it authentic. Besides, don't deny you were getting into it."

"Because I was fantasizing you were my boyfriend." It's the honest truth: When I started kissing Nathan that last time, in front of Bicky, I was totally imagining he was Avi when we were last together—which was seriously the best night of my life. After fooling around in the car didn't work, Avi and I moved onto the deserted beach. His touches and kisses and caresses were more than OMG!

"He's looking at me like he wants to kill me," Nathan complains.

"Good. Now that he's watching us, kiss me," I whisper softly, moving my lips closer to his for a repeat performance.

Nathan pries his fingers loose and steps away, although we're far enough from our other team members that nobody can hear us. "Are you kidding? First of all, didn't you sign the *Sababa* rule sheet attached to the brochure? It said, specifically, no fornicating. We're in Israel. For all I know fornicating might include kissing."

"No. It said no *going off in private* and fornicating. You really need to read the details more carefully. Anyways, nobody under the age of fifty knows the actual definition of fornicating so it won't hold up in a court of law."

"I told you I'm not doing this, Amy. Well, unless we *pretend* to date, and then after we're done with the Israeli army portion of the trip I *pretend* to break up with you and you *pretend* to be devastated in front of Tori. You can tell Tori after the fake breakup that I'm good at *everything*. You know, make me sound like the stud you know I am. You have to promise to set us up, without her knowing you're setting us up. Then you've got what you want, and I've got what I want. Deal?"

I don't mention that if he was a real stud, he wouldn't need me pretending he's one. I also don't mention that Tori hates me, so the last person she'll listen to is me. But whatever. "Fine."

Before I can think twice about my deal with Nathan, he takes my hand and leads me to the middle of where our group has assembled around Avi. Avi is standing with his arms crossed, waiting impatiently. His jaw is clenched as he watches us walk up.

"No hand holding," he barks.

Nathan gazes at me with love and tenderness, then kisses the back of my hand before letting it go.

Avi explains that we'll be racing against another team, and it's up to us to make sure everyone participates in each obstacle.

"What if I can't scale that wall?" Miranda asks.

"Have one of your teammates help you over it," Avi tells her. "You're a team. Nobody is left behind. Everyone finishes or everyone loses."

I hate races. They cause me too much stress. But Avi is a pro at this, and I'm ready to prove I'm not all talk and drama. I can kick some serious obstacle course butt when it comes right down to it.

I think.

The first heat is our team against Liron's team. I want to beat her team so bad, I can taste victory in my mouth. If only I paid more attention when they explained how to climb up that rope.

Sergeant B-S blows his trusty whistle.

We all run to the balance beam. One after another we walk across it. Next up are the monkey bars. I haven't done them since third grade, when I caught Michael Matthews looking up my pink-and-white plaid skirt. When I fell right on top of that little perv, and my knee connected with his face, I was secretly glad he went crying to Mrs. Feinstein with a bloody nose.

Tori is first. She maneuvers across the monkey bars easily enough, although she skipped the last three bars because she fell. David goes after her, skipping every other one and finishes effortlessly. Miranda's next.

"I can't do this," she tells us.

"Try," I say.

"Why try when I know I can't do it?"

She sounds more and more like me every day—it's scary. Avi said we have to do it, and work as a team, so how can she do it without actually *doing it?* I'm trying to think outside the box. It's a little hard to think when I see that four people from Liron's team have already successfully crossed the bars.

Ah, I've got it!

"What if we get on all fours and you step on our backs?"

Miranda shrugs.

I tell the team my plan. Me, Jess, Nathan, and the rest of the guys kneel down. Miranda walks on our backs while holding onto the bars above. I catch Avi nodding in approval and pointing to us as he talks to the sergeant. Miranda finishes with the bars really quickly, then profusely apologizes to the rest of the group as we each maneuver across the bars and head to the next obstacle.

Okay, so everyone finished the bars easily except for me. I got to the first bar, then slid off because my palms were sweaty and a bee buzzing in my ear freaked me out, even though I knew it was probably a worker bee. In the end, my team had to go down on their hands and knees again. I walked over them while grabbing each bar, just like Miranda.

The next obstacle is a tunnel. We all climb through easily and stop when we get to the rope. It's at least the height of a flagpole, if not higher.

I turn to my group. "I just want everyone to know that I'm afraid of heights."

"Then don't look down," Tori says. She steps on the first knot and starts climbing. "Hold it so it doesn't swing!" she yells at me.

I hold down the rope, even though I'm tempted to jiggle it hard until she falls off. I don't do it, because that would be mean. I might be whiny and a drama queen, but I like to think I'm not viciously mean to people.

David shimmies up the rope right behind Tori.

When they finish, Jess climbs and then the guys hold the rope for Miranda. For a girl who couldn't do the monkey bars, she's pretty impressive on the rope.

Now it's my turn.

Just the thought of going up that high makes me dizzy. I turn to Nathan. "Nathan, I don't think I can do it. I'll get vertigo. I don't want to die."

Nathan surveys the rope and says to me, "Well, nobody said we can't do it together. Go up and I'll follow behind you. You *are* my girlfriend; it's only natural we do it as a couple."

I roll my eyes so only Nathan can see. He kisses me on the nose, putting on the boyfriend act for anyone who cares enough to watch. When Ethan holds the bottom of the rope, I step on the first big knot.

"Go up one," Nathan instructs.

I pull myself up to the next knot, and Nathan steps on the first. His arms are wrapped around my knees, holding me tight. "You okay?"

"So far, so good."

"Go up one more," he says, loosening his hold.

I go up another one. I feel Nathan right behind me, then holding me tight again. "Any vertigo yet?"

"Not yet."

"Go up another one."

"Come on!" Tori yells. "Just do it!"

"I swear if she yells at me again I'm gonna punch her in the face. *If* I get out of this alive," I add.

"Ooh, a girl fight. What a turn-on."

"My foot is close to your nuts, Nathan, and you're suspended on a rope. It's probably not the best time to piss me off."

"You kick me in the nuts, I'm pulling your pants down," he says, following me up another section of rope.

"Avi will kill you if you do that."

"I'll already be dead from the fall so it won't matter. One more, Amy."

I close my eyes as we get higher. I have to admit, when Nathan's arms are around my knees, I feel safe.

Up and up we go. I close my eyes when I get to the top and tentatively ring the bell.

"Grab the handle and ride to the bottom," Nathan says.

"I can't."

"Yes, you can. You've come all this way—you can't stop now."

"We're losing because of you!" Tori yells at me. "What a *spaz*," I hear her say.

That's it. My anger overrides my fear. I grab the handle and shut my eyes tight while my body glides back to earth.

When my feet safely reach the ground, I open my eyes. Tori is laughing at me. Jessica looks ready to murder her, probably because she's my best friend and we always look out for each other. I storm up to the laughing hyena.

"You are seriously the most annoying person," I tell her. "I wonder how anyone can be friends with you."

She pushes me. At another time or place I might have lost my balance and fallen on my butt. But adrenaline rushes through my body, giving me strength beyond my normal capabilities. I push her back, and she goes flying. She lands on her butt.

I stand above her and let it all out. "Stop harassing me, you double-jointed, breast-challenged, designer-knockoff-wearing bully."

Tori's mouth is open wide. "You hit me!"

"No, I didn't. I pushed you."

"It's against the *Sababa* rules to assault another person. I'm telling!"

Oh, no. "You pushed me first, Tori." Geez, and they call *me* a drama queen.

Tori storms up to Avi. "Your girlfriend assaulted me."

"You've got two facts wrong. She's not my girlfriend. And you assaulted her first. Get back to the group and finish the course."

"She *pushed* me."

"This is not a discussion. Get back to the group and finish the course."

"Can't we just give up?" Nathan asks, watching as the other group nears the finish line. "We've obviously lost."

Looking into Avi's eyes, I see strength and determination. He would never give up. He won't let us give up, either. "Let's keep going until we finish," I say to my team.

We walk half-heartedly to the next obstacle.

When it's my turn to go through the swinging tire, I put my hands and feet in first. It's a big mistake, because now I'm stuck. The front half of me is through the tire, but my butt is sticking out the other end. "Push me, Nathan."

"You're giving me permission to touch your ass?"

"Not touch it. Just push it."

"Avi's watching. Should I caress it first to make him jealous?"

"Oh, yeah. What a great idea. Caressing my butt while

it's stuck in a tire is definitely going to make him jealous. *Not.*"

Nathan puts his hand on my butt. "Don't fart." He pushes me hard until I pop out of the tire. We're all sweaty and hot and it's worse because we know we lost.

The cargo net is easy enough to maneuver, although my foot slips a few times and I get rope burn on the back of my legs.

At the half wall, Miranda and I are hopeless. The guys hold Miranda on their shoulders and heave her over, then do the same for me. I swear, the wall is impossible. You have to have major arm strength to pull your body over it. Arm strength that I just don't possess.

After we step through a bunch of tires, we reach the last obstacle: crawling under the net. I look over at Avi watching us and wonder what's going through his head. There's hardly any room under the net. I kneel on the ground and duck my head. The ground is muddy, so I'm definitely getting dirty. I can't even crawl; I have to wiggle on my belly in order to go under this thing.

I use my fingernails to dig into the ground and my toes to help me slither forward like a snake. Seriously, how can Avi do the entire course in just over a half a minute?

"Push off my hands," Nathan says from behind me. He pushes me forward. I feel the time ticking away as I slide through … all the while my boobs are squished into the ground. My big C/D-cup boobs can probably fit into a training bra now.

I climb out and we all jog to the finish line. I feel victorious, although I must look like a complete mess. And we are in fact the big losers.

Avi has us sit on the ground while the other teams take their turns competing on the course. Tori grudgingly mumbles something about her uncle who's a lawyer and about what it did and did not say regarding assault in that infamous *Sababa* brochure.

Our group doesn't get to compete in the final heat because we came in last. When I look up, Avi is standing over me.

"Amy, can I talk to you for a minute?"

"Whatever you want to say to me, you can say in front of Nathan," I tell Avi. "We have no secrets between us."

Avi takes a deep breath, says, "Forget it," then walks away to stand by himself.

"He's brooding, Amy," Nathan informs me.

"I know."

I did tell Noah that whatever Avi wanted to say, he should say it to my face. Well, I guess it's time for me to hear it firsthand. I shouldn't delay the inevitable, dreaded conversation.

"Nathan, I'm going over to him."

"Want me to go with you?"

"That's probably not the safest idea. I think I can handle it." I stand, ready to face Avi and whatever news he's about to tell me. "I'll be right back."

"Good luck. You'll need it."

"What do you want to talk to me about?" I ask Avi,

who's standing close enough to our team to be seen but far enough away not to be heard.

"You didn't even try on the obstacle course, Amy."

"Are you kidding? I tried. Sorry if I'm not all buff and perfect like Liron."

"Yeah, not many girls can compete with her."

"Thanks. Next time you could give your team some pointers along the way. You *are* our team leader, you know."

"And as team leader, I knew your team could do it on your own. Amy, admit you're lying about dating Nathan."

"No."

"Then why'd you make me take you somewhere private that first day and let me kiss you?"

"I had a brain fart."

"No, you're having a brain fart right now by pretending you and Nathan are a couple. God is definitely inscribing you in the Book of Liars."

My blood is way past boiling now. "How dare you! I'll have you know that Nathan's kisses are the best I've ever had. By far. You could take lessons from him."

He opens his mouth to respond, then snaps it shut when someone walks by. We can't have a conversation in true private and Avi hates dishing his dirt in public. "When are you gonna stop playing games, Amy?"

"Never. I like games. It makes life interesting. You should try it sometime, you know."

"I don't have time for games." He looks behind me to Nathan, who's chatting with Miranda and Jessica. "So this is how you want to end it?"

"Don't you?"

"No. Didn't you talk to Noah?"

"Not about us. Listen, Avi, you and I both know it's not working."

"I'm not good at relationships, Amy."

"Well, that's one more obstacle we'd have to get through if we were dating. You'd have to deal with my games, and with your girlfriend being an obstacle-course flunkee. I'd have to deal with your commitment phobia and the fact that you don't really want a full-time girlfriend you have to answer to. We were doomed from the start."

He lets out a slow breath. "Please don't make more out of this than it is. I've been trying to be who you want me to be, Amy."

"I just want you to be *yourself.* I've never once asked you to be someone else. It may not seem like it now, but I'm actually doing you a favor. Now you can have Liron or any other girl all to yourself, with a clear conscience."

Nathan slides up beside me and puts his arm around my shoulders. "Sorry, Avi," he says. "You win some, you lose some."

Liron comes up out of nowhere and stands next to Avi. She nudges him. "So you told her?"

He nods.

"I'm so sorry, Amy," Liron says so sincerely I want to rip those blond streaks right out of her head. "But I'm glad you know. Now I won't feel so weird around you anymore."

Great. That makes one of us.

Avi puts his arm around Liron. I want to swat it off her, but as Nathan said, you win some, you lose some.

I just wish I wasn't the one who'd lost.

14

At night, I'm so shaken up by the finality of our break-up that I skip my normal facial cleansing routine and just climb into bed. Avi and I have broken up before, but this time it's for real. I try sleeping, but with the squeaky springs above me (Vic's indentation getting more and more pronounced), along with the fact that I can't get the awful conversation Avi and I had at the obstacle course out of my mind, sleeping is impossible. Listen, deep down I know I should have come clean to Avi about my non-relationship with Nathan. But I couldn't.

Avi uses a rifle, Krav Maga, and non-communication for self-defense. I use games, attitude, and manipulation.

No matter what I've thought in the past, we might just be too different.

In the morning, our team gets assigned kitchen duty, (thanks to Tori and her tirade yesterday on the obstacle course). It's not bathroom-cleaning duty, so I'm okay with it. Again, they wake us up at the crack of dawn. Actually, it's before the crack of dawn, because it's still pitch black outside. My team is held back while everyone else does an activity. Ronit leads us to the kitchen, and even though I don't want to see Avi, I can't help scanning the base looking for him. He's nowhere in sight.

Noah, the American IDF soldier from Colorado, is in the kitchen waiting for us.

"Hey, Noah," I groan, my eyes still at half-mast.

"Hey. I'm going to give you assignments." He points to a humongous pot half the size of me. "Two of you need to set baskets of bread on the tables. Two of you need to put water in that pot. When it boils, put three hundred eggs inside and let them sit in the boiling water for fifteen minutes. Two of you need to put jam in the bowls. And two of you need to make coffee."

We divvy up the jobs.

As soon as Miranda and I start pulling jars of jam from the huge refrigerator, bees swarm around us.

"Noah, the bees are bothering us," I tell him.

Noah waves some of the bees away. "Yeah, that's kind of a hazard of working here. Living with bees becomes part of your daily life."

"I hate bees," Miranda tells him.

"You also hate me," I blurt out.

"I can't believe you just said that."

"Why not? It's true."

Miranda huffs and walks over to talk about me or complain about me to Jessica. I just want Miranda to tell me what I did to piss her off so much. If I don't know what it is, I can't fix it any more than I can fix what went wrong with Avi.

Noah helps me pull more jars of jam out of the fridge. "What's her problem?"

"I wish I knew."

Noah shakes his head. "I keep my expectations low, so nobody disappoints me."

"Yeah, well, I have high expectations." I look toward Miranda. "I guess my friends do, too."

"Expectations make people miserable, so whatever yours are, lower them. You'll definitely be happier." Noah waves his hand around, gesturing to the entire kitchen. "You think I wanted to be assigned kitchen duties? Nope. But to be honest, at least it's quiet and the biggest pests I have to deal with here are the bees. Besides, I'm only here for three months and then I'm getting transferred to another base to get trained as an instructor. It's all good."

"You're a better person than me."

Listen, I know who I am and what my strengths are. And my strengths do not include having little or no expectations. I guess I shouldn't be surprised, then, when people let me down.

After Noah leaves me alone for a minute with instructions about how to ladle spoonfuls of jam into the plastic bowls, I'm having trouble fending off the four bees hovering around me. You'd think dropping globs of the jam would be easy, but it's not. It's sticky and messy and two of the bees just got stuck in the jam.

"Umm ... Noah ... I think there's a problem."

Noah is at my side. Miranda is right behind him, so I guess he was able to coax her back over here. "What's the jam?" he asks, then laughs. "Get it. What's the *jam*? You're scooping the *jam*."

You gotta love it when someone laughs at their own jokes.

"Yeah, I don't know how to break the news to you, but a few bees are stuck in the jam," I tell him.

"Just pick 'em out before you set the bowls on the tables," he says, as if it happens every day. He doesn't even peer in the bowls to see the annoying stinging creatures struggling for their lives. That's what they get for hovering around the jam, I guess.

Noah leaves Miranda and me to fish out the bees while he helps Eli and David with the eggs.

I look down into the first bowl of jam. I can do this. I'm trying to think about the consequences of an IDF soldier, jam on his bread, biting into a little bee corpse as a bonus treat. At least they're not those fuzzy bees, because having a mouthful of that fuzz would definitely not go over well.

I spot a bee in the next bowl. With shaky hands, I slowly

fish it out with a spoon and flick it into the garbage can. "This is so gross," I say to nobody in particular, since my partner Miranda is pretty much ignoring me and everyone else is doing other tasks.

Within five minutes I've inspected and de-bee'd eleven bowls. I look into the twelfth bowl and find the next bee. Seriously, don't bees have eyes and see their cousins and brothers drowning in the sticky stuff? You'd think they'd be smart enough to stay away, but no. Their little bee brains aren't equipped with street smarts.

I slowly fish out another bee and head for the garbage can. The bee is still alive—I can see it walking in the jam on my spoon. Eww. I suppress a gag. If it crawls anywhere near my hand, I'm dropping the spoon and running out of here.

I'm almost to the garbage can when I feel a sharp pain on my butt. "Ahhhh!" I scream, whipping myself around to see what or who was the cause. But instead of it being an insect like I suspected, it's Nathan. With his thumb and pointer finger in a pinching position. My fake boyfriend just pinched my ass.

"How's my sweetie?" he asks, raising and lowering his eyebrows at me. Tori is beside him, giving me the evil eye.

Speaking of sweet mixed with evil, I examine the jam/bee on the spoon in my hand.

Oh. No.

The jam isn't there. Neither is the bee. I quickly scan the floor, but it's not there. I frantically scan my shirt. Sure enough, there's a big glob of jam on my sleeve. The bee is stuck in it, creepily walking in the jam. "Get it off! Get it off! Eww!"

Nathan takes my elbow, looks up at me and says in a sexy voice, "Let me get that for you." He checks to make sure Tori is watching him be my hero. I expect him to flick it off me, but instead his tongue snakes out as he leans close to the jam … and the bee.

I quickly realize he thinks he's only licking jam off my sleeve.

"Nathan, don't…"

"I'm here for you, babycakes." Before I can pull away, he licks off the jam and struggling bee with the tip of his tongue.

My hand flies over my mouth. "Oh, my God. Nathan—you just ate a bee!"

Nathan's face contorts in shock, and I realize I didn't have to tell him he ate a bee. He figured it out all by himself. "Ow! What the fu—"

He runs to the garbage can faster than I've ever seen him move and spits jam and the bee out of his mouth.

"Nathan, are you allergic to bees?" Miranda cries out over the commotion.

"No."

There's a sigh of relief that Nathan isn't going to die. I've never heard so many swear words come out of his mouth at one time since I've known him.

I rub his back as he rinses his tongue in the big metal kitchen sink. "I'm so sorry. I tried to warn you—"

"It sthung my tung. Thit," he swears. He sticks his tongue out and points. "Take de sthinger outh."

"Okay." I examine his tongue. "What should I be looking for?"

"The sthinger!"

Is it white? Red? Black? I've never taken out a stinger before. I'm frantic with worry.

"His tongue is swollen," Miranda says. "I think he needs to go to the infirmary."

"Miranda's right," I cry out. "Nathan, I'm so sorry."

"You're thorry? Amy, thath's the lasth thime I'm pinthing your assth."

"Stop talking, Nathan. Your throat might swell up so bad it'll stop the oxygen."

Nathan opens his mouth wide and breathes in and out, proving his throat is letting enough air through.

"Close your mouth, Nathan," Tori says. "You look like a damn fish gasping for air, you dork."

"Uthually I'm thexy," Nathan tells her, then nudges me to intervene.

"The *sexiest*," I agree, but I don't think Tori is buying it.

Noah leads Nathan, who's now screaming unintelligible obscenities, all the way to the infirmary. Great. Now I've ruined my fake boyfriend's reputation, too.

Tori finishes the task of piling plastic coffee mugs on a tray.

"Hey, Tori. I thought you said these were worker bees that don't sting," I say to her.

"I didn't say they won't sting if you *eat* them," she

responds, then walks back out into the dining area with the tray of coffee mugs.

I follow her with a tray of jam-filled bowls. "It's too bad my boyfriend won't be able to kiss me because of his bee sting."

"Your problem, not mine," she says, attitude dripping from each word.

I set two bowls on each table, wondering how I'm going to make her go out with Nathan after we "break up" and I'm supposedly devastated. "Who do you like?"

"As if I'm gonna tell you."

Seriously, this girl is so one-dimensional you'd think when she turns sideways she'd be as flat as a piece of paper. She belongs on another planet. "You know, it wouldn't hurt if you acted a little nicer."

"Why should I? Acting nice didn't get me anywhere. It sure didn't keep my parents together, that's for sure."

"Are they divorced?"

"That's none of your business. Just leave me alone."

I'm shocked. Tori actually opened up to me. The good part is that I now know what her deal is. She's not mad at me, per se. Okay, so I'm sure I annoy her 10 percent of the time. But the real issue behind her pissy face and bitchy attitude is a daughter who wants her parents to get together and doesn't see it happening any time soon.

"Not that you care, but I know how you feel," I tell her.

"I doubt it. Are *your* parents divorced?"

"No, worse. My parents were never married. How

would you like growing up knowing you were the result of a one-night stand? That's my reality. And no matter how much attitude I have, that will never change."

"But you have friends. I have nobody."

"If you'd act a little nicer maybe we could be friends. If you stop calling me a spaz every two minutes, that might be a start."

"What makes you think even if I wanted a friend, I'd pick you? Besides, you *are* a spaz." Tori tosses her hair with a flick of her wrist, showing me a flash of dark hair underneath her blond locks, and stomps back to the kitchen.

She ignores me the rest of the time as she busies herself with one task or another. I guess now is not the time to become buddy-buddy with her, especially when she's in charge of the hot coffee. It's not a level playing field.

Avi walks in the door and I almost drop a bowl of jam. I wish I could forget the long talks we'd have on the phone when he was on military leave. Or that his hands are strong enough to dig ditches in record time and gentle enough to caress my skin and make me beg for more.

"Where's Noah?" he asks in a businesslike tone, as if I'm someone he just met.

"He took Nathan to the infirmary," I answer back, just as businesslike.

"Why?"

"Nathan kind of ate a live bee."

"Kind of? How does someone *kind of* eat a bee?"

"It's a long story," I say, not wanting to get into it.

Tori appears by Avi's side. "He licked it off her. You know, with his tongue." As if Avi can't get the visual, Tori sticks her tongue out and wiggles it up and down.

So much for the conversation staying businesslike. I have a vindictive urge to pull her tongue until it comes out of her mouth.

Avi looks as if he's about to be ill. "I get the picture. No need to demonstrate."

Avi and I meet up again at the tray full of bread baskets. I figure I need to explain, so I tap him on the arm. When his dark gaze meets mine, I step back. I can't think straight when I'm looking directly into his eyes.

"Um, yeah. The way Tori told you what happened isn't really how it went down."

"I don't need details."

"But I want to explain." I pretend to be busy picking up baskets of bread to set on the tables as I talk, sparing myself from looking directly at him. "So, um, there were bees stuck in the jam. And when Nathan pinched my butt *by accident*, I twirled around and jam landed on my sleeve. He licked it off, not knowing there was a bee stuck in it."

"He didn't do anything by accident, Amy. Tell Nathan to keep his hands off your *tachat*. And while he's at it, tell him to keep his tongue away from you, too."

"You jealous?"

"Why should I be? I have Liron, right?"

"Right. And I have Nathan, right?"

He shrugs. "I don't know, you tell me. You've obviously had his tongue down your throat multiple times."

Oh, that was low. How dare he turn this around and make me the bad person, when he's probably been playing "battling tongues" with Liron! "Yeah, well, he might be tongue-challenged at the moment, but normally he's *the best*." I emphasize the last two words for effect. If Avi's tight, white knuckles are any indication, I think I've accomplished my goal.

"Amy?" He says, his voice laced with frustration.

I cross my arms on my chest (actually under my chest, because my boobs are so big). "What?" I know we're about to have it out, right here in the middle of the IDF cafeteria.

The door between the kitchen and dining area opens. It's Jess and Ethan, bringing out the baskets of bread. Both stop in their tracks, obviously sensing the massive amount of tension in the room.

"Everything okay in here?" Jess asks.

I narrow my eyes at Avi. "It's all peachy. Avi and I were just discussing the art of a good kiss."

"While that might be fascinating at another time, we have baskets of bread we need to put out. Help us," Jess says.

I see something, out of the corner of my eye, on one of the pieces of bread in the basket Jess is holding. "There are a couple of ants crawling on the bread."

Jess shrugs. "Noah said to consider them spices."

15

Insects, whether they're bees or ants,
should not be eaten alive.

Breakfast is half over when Nathan reappears.

"How's your tongue?" Miranda asks once he reaches our table.

Nathan shrugs. Noah is standing behind him. "He says it hurts to talk. The nurse told him the swelling should go down in a few hours."

"That's what you get for pinching my butt. God was punishing you."

He gives me the finger as he takes a seat beside me.

"God's gonna punish you for that, too."

Across the table, Miranda slams down her cup of milk. It splashes all over her uniform, but I don't think she notices.

"Amy, leave him alone. Don't you think he's dealing with enough without you making him feel worse?"

"I was just kidding, Miranda."

"Yeah, well..." Miranda looks around, realizing she's causing a scene. Miranda's not used to creating drama. Her voice shakes as she says, "Maybe Nathan doesn't know you're kidding."

"Nathan and I joke around all the time. We always do."

Nathan puts his arm around me, nods, and smiles.

"Oh," Miranda says, slowly sitting back down. She doesn't look up until we're done eating and dismissed from breakfast.

On the way back to the barracks, I catch up to Miranda. "I know why you're pissed with me. You have the hots for Nathan."

She glances sideways at me. "So?"

Wow, I'm right. I mean, I got the idea when she went all ballistic on me, milk splattered on her face during breakfast. But I still can't believe it.

"I'm not really dating him, you know."

Miranda stops and turns to me. "Then who are you dating, Amy? Because you seem to be dating guys you hate, and hating guys you date, and hating girls who like the guys you date, or hate, and—"

My brain is on overload. "You lost me. I'm confused."

"That makes two of us." She stomps away from me.

I hurry to catch up. "What do you want me to do? I hate you being mad at me."

"I don't know. I have no claim to Nathan. He doesn't even like me."

"Are you double-jointed?"

"What?"

"Are you double-jointed?"

"No. In case you haven't noticed, I'm fat and had to step on people's backs in order to complete the monkey bars at the obstacle course."

"So did I. And you're not fat, Miranda."

She picks up her shirt and grabs her bulging stomach. "What do you call this?" To be honest, I've seen people way bigger.

Umm… Umm… "I call it 'extra.'"

"Extra what?"

Oh, I hate being put in a corner I can't get out of gracefully. "Just 'extra'."

She pulls her shirt down. "Well, I call it *fat*. Nathan isn't going to like me. Did you see his last girlfriend, Bicky? She was rail thin."

"Miranda, she was a druggie. That kind of thin is *not* attractive."

"Neither is this extra thirty pounds I carry around. And no matter how much I try to get rid of it, I can't. Because I crave sweets, and once I start eating I can't stop. Do you know what it's like not to be able to stop doing something you know isn't good for you?"

"Sure I do."

She puts her hand on her hip, totally unconvinced.

"Well, I know I do and say things that hurt other people," I tell her. "I can't stop it sometimes. It's a protective thing. You know, so I hurt people before they have a chance to hurt me. Don't let anyone else know, but I've got issues."

"Everybody has issues, Amy." She sighs.

I guess she's right. Tori has issues from her parents' divorce, Miranda has weight/image issues, I have emotional protection/ego issues, Jess has hypochondriac issues...

Is anyone human actually normal?

I'm beginning to think being normal is actually *abnormal*.

16

Zits are God's way of making sure we know we're only human and far from perfect.
I'd just like him to remind me a little less often.

Looking at my face in the bathroom mirror the next morning, I'm horrified. I stare at the small zit I noticed last night after I took a shower. The small red bump appeared above my left eyebrow. It's not small anymore.

Jessica is brushing her teeth at the sink next to me. "Don't touch it," she says as she wipes her mouth with a towel and places her toothbrush in a plastic tube she brought from home. "If you do, it'll just get worse and take longer to go away. Use cover-up and forget about it. Give it two or three days, and it'll be gone."

She walks out of the bathroom and I take another look in the mirror. Two or three days? Ugh. I tentatively touch it. It hurts. And it's so big it deserves its own name.

George the Zit.

George is being stubborn. Well, I'm stubborn too. I don't listen to Jess and I try and get rid of George myself by squeezing him away. But now George looks worse and has started to throb. It looks like a bright red radish has imbedded itself on my forehead.

If I had bangs, I could hide George from the rest of the world. But I don't. I head to the barracks with my hand over George and sneak past Jess. Lifting my makeup case, I pull out my trusty cover-up. But as I pat it on and examine it in my small travel mirror, the cover-up looks like caked-on silly putty. Besides, when I sweat the stuff is going to come right off. So I do the next best thing: I pull out my travel first-aid kit and cover George up with one of those round Band-Aids. When George is hidden from the world, I head to the courtyard to wait for Ronit to order us into formation.

Nathan is outside, his tongue fully recovered from the bee incident.

"What the hell happened to your forehead?" Nathan asks with a grimace. I swear he says it so loud everyone within a mile can hear him.

"Nothing," I say, hoping against all hope he'll drop the subject.

"I've got two theories," he says. "Either you cut yourself shaving your monobrow, or you're covering up a huge zit."

"Shut up or I'll make you eat another bee."

"Hi, Nathan," Miranda says.

"Let me guess what's for breakfast," Jessica says as she walks up to us. "Ant-encrusted toast, hard-boiled eggs, and delicious bee-jam." Her voice trails off after a glance at my forehead. I'm trying to look the other way, but she grabs my arm. "Amy, please tell me you didn't touch it."

"I didn't touch it," I say roughly. I'm not lying. I didn't touch it, I *mutilated* it.

Nathan pretends to cough, but I know he's laughing. "She's got a big zit she's covering up but is too embarrassed to admit it. Come on, Amy, fess up," he says, then reaches over to pull the Band-Aid off.

I slap his hand away.

"How big *is* it?" Miranda asks.

"I told you to leave it alone," Jess scolds.

"Okay, okay everyone!" I yell, then pull the Band-Aid off and point to my forehead. "Everyone, meet George."

Nathan pretends to gag. "That looks so *nasty*, Amy. What the *hell* did you do to it?"

"You named your zit?" Miranda asks.

"I figured since George and I are going to be together for a while, he might as well have a name," I tell her, ignoring Nathan. Jess is still staring at my forehead as if she's not quite sure how I managed to turn tiny George into big, red, angry George.

Nathan is laughing again.

"Does it look really bad?" I ask my friends.

Nathan gives me a resounding "Yes!"

Miranda shrugs and nods at the same time.

Jess says, "They might make you go to the infirmary for fear it's something contagious."

I slap my hand over my forehead and run back to the barracks. Unfortunately, Tori is still in the room.

"We're supposed to be outside in less than a minute," Tori says.

"So leave." I pull out my mirror and look up at Tori. "Do you mind? I need some privacy."

"For what?"

"It's a long story that has to do with a big zit I named George."

I examine George in the mirror. Unfortunately, Tori sees him too. Her lips curl up in disgust. "Eww."

"I know. You want to call me a spaz again because I have a zit?"

"No. But you better go out there before you get in trouble for being late."

George looks nastier than before. "What am I gonna do?"

Tori shrugs. "Put on a hat."

"I don't even know where mine is. Besides, George might get infected from rubbing against the material."

"I could cut you some bangs, if you want," Tori says. "My mom's a hairdresser."

"Really?"

"Really. Your face structure would actually look good with bangs."

"You'd really cut me bangs?"

"Anything to get you to stop looking at yourself in the mirror." She pulls out scissors from her duffle and slides my hair through her fingers. "Trust me."

She has no clue how hard that is for me, but Rabbi Glassman says that sometimes it helps to make people feel needed. "I trust you," I tell her.

"Thanks for sharing your story about your parents when we had kitchen duty," she says as she snips away. "I see you with all the stuff you have, and I think you have the perfect life."

"It's my parents' way of making up for their shortcomings."

"There. I'm done." She puts the scissors down and holds up the mirror so I can inspect my new *do*.

I never really wanted bangs. I was six years old the last time I had bangs, and they feel weird brushing up against my forehead. I have to admit they don't look half bad.

Outside, sure enough, everyone is in formation. Tori and I come sauntering out. Sergeant B-S isn't here, thank goodness. But Avi is.

All eyes turn to Avi.

"Why are you late?" he asks us.

"It's my fault, not Tori's," I tell him. "It was a medical issue."

"Are you sick?" he asks, his voice laced with concern that makes my knees weak. He cocks his head and inspects me, looking for a wound or weakness.

"Not exactly."

"Do you have a fever?"

To my horror, he picks his hand up and is about to feel my forehead. I jump back, afraid he'll find George. "No!"

"Amy, my patience is wearing thin. Fast."

I can tell. "It's not a fever. Tori was cutting my hair."

"Since when is cutting hair a medical issue?"

"It just is."

Avi looks up to the sky, probably asking God for the strength to deal with me. I don't blame him. Truth is, I *am* a spaz.

"Tori, get back in formation. Amy, give me twenty push-ups."

"Can I do girlie ones?"

"No."

"I can't do guy's ones. I don't have enough upper arm strength."

"Yes, you do." He points to the ground. "Stop stalling."

I stretch out on the ground. Thankfully we're on a paved sidewalk so I don't have little pebbles sticking into my palms.

With my hands on either side of my shoulders and the tips of my toes on the pavement, I straighten my arms.

I look up, and stare straight into Avi's eyes. He's squatting right in front of me. For him, pushups are no big deal. For me, on the other hand...

"Stop thinking and just do them," he says softly so no one else can hear. "Pretend your body is a piece of wood and your elbows are hinges." He gets in position and demonstrates it for me.

I bend my elbows a tiny bit and straighten them.

"That's not a pushup, Amy."

"It is for me."

"Go down farther." He demonstrates it again, reminding me of when I did them in front of Sergeant B-S my first night here.

I look into his eyes, which have determination written all over them.

"I wouldn't ask you to do something you couldn't do," he says. "Push yourself."

The thing is, I want to make Avi proud of me. And if he says I can do it, maybe I can.

I bend my elbows again, all the while trying to keep the rest of my body straight. My boobs are almost touching the ground when I straighten.

"That's it. Nineteen more," Avi says, doing them right along with me.

I do two more, my arms shaking and struggling each time. Going down isn't the problem; it's the pushing up part.

"Seventeen more."

I take a deep breath. My arms are tired. I'm not mad at Avi for punishing me. It's my own fault for being so vain. I look up, wishing everyone wasn't watching.

"I have faith in you," Avi says softly. "No matter what, I always have."

Now I want to cry, because he probably has more faith in me than I have in myself. As I lower my body again, Avi's determination makes me do more pushups. Every time I think I'm going to collapse, I look up into his beautiful milk-chocolate eyes for strength.

Sweat is dripping off my forehead. My shirt is wet from sweat and I probably smell, but I finish my twenty pushups and stand up.

"You'd be a great soldier if you didn't complain all the time."

I shrug. "And you'd be a great boyfriend if you didn't kiss other girls."

17

---

*Running should be saved for times
when you're being chased.*

After we sit through another classroom session on rifle safety and have dinner, we're informed that we'll be going on a night run.

"Like a Taco Bell run?" I ask. "Fun." Although I've never seen a Taco Bell in Israel, I've seen a few McDonald's. I had a McKebab at one last summer, with *cheeps* on the side (which is really just French fries).

Ronit and Liron look at each other in confusion. "What's a Taco Bell run?"

"You know... a food run."

Liron laughs. "We weren't talking about a food run. We mean *night run* literally."

"Where you run at night," Ronit adds, just in case I don't get it.

"Oh."

If I'm to be completely honest, the last thing I want to do at nine p.m. is run. In fact, the last thing I ever want to do is run, period. I'd hate running if it was at nine at night or nine in the morning (or three in the afternoon, for that matter).

At nine on the dot, just when the sun has almost left us, we congregate in a big, open area right outside the base. I spot Nathan and pull him aside. "Nathan, don't you think Miranda's awesome?"

"Uh, yeah. Why?"

"I was just wondering if you, you know, would ever consider her as more than a friend. You know, like girl-friend material."

"No. She's too serious. And too nice."

"Nice is a good trait, Nathan."

"Yeah, *in a friend*. I like Miranda *as a friend*. Get it? I need a raunchy and inappropriate girl … you know, some-one I consider a challenge."

"I got it." Tori's the one.

Nathan shrugs. "Truth is, I know Miranda's had a crush on me for months. I tried thinking of her that way, but it didn't work. The yin/yang thing just isn't there. I feel bad about it, if that makes you feel any better."

I sigh, knowing that pairing my two friends isn't going to work. "Well, as long as you feel bad about it, I guess you're off the hook."

"What are you wearing on your head?" Sergeant B-S asks me, cutting my conversation with Nathan short.

I reach up and feel the hot-pink headlight my mom bought me for the trip. At the time I thought it was lame to wear a flashlight strapped to your forehead, but when I got ready for the night run that has nothing to do with food or Taco Bell, I put it on. "A flashlight."

"Who told you to put it on?"

"Nobody. I thought of it all by myself. It'll help me see where I'm going."

Sergeant B-S takes the flashlight off my head. "A flashlight in a real military operation would give away your location."

"This isn't a real military operation," I say, stating the obvious.

"We're simulating one. No flashlights. Use the moon as your light." He hands my flashlight back to me and faces the rest of the unit. "In a real operation, troops move at night. Since there are only a few hours of darkness, you have to move fast so the enemy is taken by surprise."

Four guys are chosen to carry a stretcher while they run, with four more guys as backup stretcher-holders. Nathan is one of the backups. Two other guys are assigned to carry what they call "jerry cans," which are water-filled jugs, on their backs.

The rest of us wait to be led on our run. I don't know what to do with my headlight, so I strap it on my head and turn the light off. Yes, I'm aware it looks ridiculous, but at least it covers up George.

Sergeant B-S points to the front of the line. "Stretcher people, move up front. People with jerry cans are next. Then slow runners and then good runners."

"Why are good runners last?" I question.

"So they can help the runners who aren't so fast," Liron informs us. "We're only as good as our slowest runner."

"I need a volunteer," Sergeant B-S barks out.

Yeah, right. As *if.* Jess and I look at each other knowingly. We've been warned not to volunteer. Especially when we don't even know what we're volunteering for. Plus, I'm dreading running at night as it is ... the last thing I need to do is carry something as well. I have my big boobs to carry, which is more than enough for one person to handle.

Since nobody raises their hand, Sergeant B-S walks among us to pick the unlucky person for the mysterious task. I learned a long time ago that you lessen your chances of being picked if you don't make eye contact with the picker. I concentrate on my fingernails instead, as if I find my cuticles the most interesting things I've ever laid my eyes on.

Out of the corner of my eye I see Sergeant B-S moving in front of me. I hold my breath and pray he passes me.

He does. Phew.

But he stops right in front of Jessica. "You," he says.

Oh, no. Poor Jess.

"Me?" Jess chokes out.

"Move to the front of the line. You'll be carried on the stretcher, as the pretend-wounded."

Jess's eyes light up. "So I don't have to run?"

"No."

"Cool!" Jess gives me an excited look before taking her place on the stretcher. I watch in envy as the stretcher-carriers lift her up.

The line starts moving, and already I feel like I'm in the Chicago Marathon. I sure hope we won't be running 26.2 miles. We start out at a slow jog on the paved road, but then the front of the line gains momentum and speed just as we're led up some rocky areas.

Jess is lying down, enjoying a ride on a stretcher, while I'm running with a dorky unlit headlight strapped to my head. Avi is bringing up the rear with Nimrod. They're both in full military gear again, with vests, rifles, and everything, which is probably heavier than the jerry cans.

The area gets steeper and steeper. We're running up a mountain. I wonder if, when I get to the top, I can just roll down. Soon I'm struggling to keep up. Miranda has fallen behind, and I hear Nimrod urging her on.

I try to drink from my canteen, but it all spills down my neck and the front of my shirt because it's not easy to drink and run at the same time.

I'm not a fast runner, and when the good runners catch up to me, I get frustrated. Especially because I see Jess in the distance, lying on the stretcher like Cleopatra being carried by her manservants.

When I'm sweating and panting and think I can't run anymore, Avi's words from earlier echo in my head. *Push yourself. I have faith in you.*

I run faster, the mantra helping me along. I feel victorious when I catch up to the guys running with the jerry cans.

Avi's right. I can do this. My arms are moving fast, my legs are moving fast, and I'm ignoring the fact that my canteen is banging against my side with every stride. I think of all the soldiers who have it worse, like everyone in the Sayeret Tzefa unit. They have to carry a big rifle, wear a heavy vest, and still run.

I'm a machine now, running fast without thinking about how much I hate it or want to go to sleep. I'm not thinking about Avi, or George the Zit, or Nathan, or Tori, or Miranda, or even Jess aka Cleopatra…I am one with the earth.

Except…

My toe hits what must be a rock, stopping my momentum. I'm gonna fall. I try to get my hands out to break the impact, but my reflexes aren't as fast as my feet.

I slam to the ground. I'm not lucky enough to fall on pavement or grass—just gravel and stones. My hips get slammed against sharp rocks. Pebbles slice into my forearms as I slide over them. As my chin scrapes the ground like a plane landing on a runway, my headlight slides off George and crashes onto the bridge of my nose, blocking my view.

Damn. That. Hurt.

My body is paralyzed from shock and pain. I'm afraid to move. My forearms are burning like someone has lit a match, and the flames are licking my skin.

Some people have passed me, but others have stopped. There's commotion. At least I haven't fainted, which is a good thing.

"Are you okay?" someone asks.

"She totally wiped out," someone else adds.

"Amy!" It's Avi's voice. He doesn't sound like a military commando anymore. He sounds concerned. His concern, along with the burning in my arms and knees and chin, makes me emotional. As I swallow back tears, a warm, comforting hand pulls off my headlight and pushes the hair out of my face. "Amy, can you move?"

I dread the thought of moving. I'd rather stay here for a while because I fear the additional injuries I've gotten and don't know about yet. "I think so," I say, wincing as I attempt, and fail, to sit up. "Oh, God, I'm *so* embarrassed."

Avi orders the gawkers to keep going. Nimrod urges the unit forward and leaves Avi to tend to my injuries.

"Everyone's gone. It's just us."

"Aren't we going to get in trouble if we're alone?" I sniff a couple of times, then wipe my nose with my sleeve. I'm giving up preserving my ego. In fact, my ego is non-existent now ... I think I left it back in Chicago.

"It's fine. I'm trained in first aid."

I swipe away the tears running down my cheeks as Avi slowly helps me sit up.

"I'm fine," I say, sniffing again. "I need to get up so I can finish the run."

"You're not doing anything until I know the extent of your injuries."

I push his hands away as he pulls up my now shredded sleeves. "Stop."

"Don't be stubborn, Amy." I try to stand, but Avi pushes me back down. He swears when he bends my elbow and sees the damage. "You're hurt. There's blood all over your arms."

"It doesn't matter. If you got your arm shot off, you'd jump right up and finish the run because you're superhuman."

"I'm not superhuman."

"Sure you are. Liron is, too."

He stops his examination and looks at me. "Huh?"

"She's the female version of you. If she fell, she'd jump up and finish this stupid running exercise on these stupid rocks that jut out of the stupid ground without warning."

"That's a lot of stupids," he says.

"Yeah, well, that's how I feel right now. Like everything is stupid." I feel my hot, stupid tears streaming down my dirty, dusty face.

"I need to clean out your stupid wounds with some stupid water. Okay?" He pours water from his canteen on my arms.

I suck in my breath. "Ow. Ow. Ow. Ow."

"Sorry. Just hang in there." He unzips a pocket on his vest and takes out what I guess is first aid stuff. He rips open a packet and pulls out a little white antiseptic pad.

I jerk my arm away in anticipation of the antiseptic on my open wounds. "Ouch!" I say before he even touches me with it. "It's gonna sting."

"Only for a second. It'll help numb it, too. Trust me."

I give him a "yeah, right" look.

"Trust me," he says, so tenderly it rocks my insides.

He takes one arm and gently wipes the cloth over my wound. When I wince, he softly blows on the cut, easing the sting. I close my eyes and try to focus on the pain instead of his breath and his fingers touching my skin.

Feeling his soft breath makes me think about when we were under the blanket on the couch at my condo. His kisses started at my lips, trailed over my skin, and then his breath followed those kisses ... and then his tongue followed that same path, giving me goose bumps. When he stopped, I begged him to do it again and again. And he did.

"The last thing I want is a female version of me," he says as he's busy pulling out another antiseptic pad. He takes my other arm and cleans it, blowing on it gently like before. It feels so good I never want him to stop. My anger at him weakens with each touch of his hand and each whisper of his breath on my skin. I hope he doesn't notice.

He bandages both my forearms with gauze. "It's only a temporary fix until I get you to the infirmary, but it'll have to do. What else hurts?"

"Everything. My hips are burning, my knees are burning. My chin feels raw." Even my heart hurts—being this close to him and knowing that our relationship is over stabs like a knife. I moan.

"Does anything feel like it's broken?" he asks, his arm supporting my back.

"No." Nothing besides my heart, but that had nothing to do with my fall.

He pushes up my pants leg, and his fingers run over my knee checking the damage. He makes me bend and straighten my leg a couple of times. "No cuts or broken bones, but you're gonna have some nasty bruises tomorrow."

I take a deep breath, gulping back tears. My breath comes out in little spurts. I hate showing this much weakness, especially in front of someone who protects his own at all costs. "Thanks for helping me, Avi."

He rubs my chin with another pad. He cups my cheeks in his hands and swipes my tears away with his thumbs. "I'm your team leader. You're my responsibility."

Duh! I should've known he wasn't being this nice because he still cared about me. I hold back a response. Time stops, though, as being this close brings back a flood of emotions. Avi leans forward, and I wonder whether, if I lean in, we'll kiss. I turn away before I'm tempted to try it. What if he turns away and my lips connect with his cheek? I'd die from embarrassment.

He packs up the unused gauze and the open packets. "I'm taking you back to the base now," he says, lifting me up and carrying me in his strong, protective arms.

While it's so tempting to lean my head into his neck and let him take care of me, his words from this morning are still echoing in my head.

"Avi, I want to finish the run." I swear I can almost hear my bruised body scream "*no!*" But I want to push myself. I want to prove to myself, to Avi, and to my entire unit that I'm a warrior woman. Back when we were digging ditches, Liron accused Avi of taking it easy on me. And as much as I feel happy and safe in Avi's arms, and would love to be carried down the mountain because my body is protesting every movement I make, I don't want to give up.

He slowly puts me down. "You don't have to."

"I know. But you told me this morning to push myself."

He shakes his head and points to my torn pants and shirt. "Not while you're bleeding and hurt."

I show him my gauze-covered arms. "Would you run even if you were bleeding?"

"Probably."

"Would Liron do it?"

"Probably. But she's been training alongside us Sayeret Tzefa trainees."

"Yeah, well, if she can do it, so can I." I strap on my canteen and slide my hot-pink headlight onto my head. I must look ridiculous with torn clothes, a scraped-up chin, and a hot-pink light that I'm not allowed to turn on, but I've got determination on my side. "I'm a kick-ass Jewish warrior woman and don't you forget it."

"I won't," he says, smiling as we start at a slow jog up

the mountain to try and catch up with everyone else. "I'm looking forward to seeing how a kick-ass Jewish warrior woman does at live-fire rifle shooting tomorrow."

Huh? "Live fire?"

"What? You didn't think you were learning M16 rifle safety in the classroom for nothing, did you?"

Umm...

18

Sometimes I'm a kick-ass Jewish warrior woman...
and sometimes I'm not.

Everyone is totally surprised when Avi and I catch up to
them on the night run. There's a big bonfire, and everyone
is sitting around it. Sergeant B-S walks up to Avi and me
and says something in Hebrew, which is obviously about
me because Avi gestures to my torn uniform and scraped-
up chin when he answers.

"You don't want to go back to the base?" Sergeant B-S
asks.

"No." I have to admit I'm still in some pain, but whatever numbing stuff was on that pad Avi used on my arms
has taken the edge off.

Sergeant B-S nods approvingly. "Gefen, make sure she
gets checked when we get back."

Avi salutes the sergeant.

The bonfire lights up the area and spreads warmth into the cool desert air. I could point out to Sergeant B-S that if my headlight could alert the enemy to our location, a big bonfire would most likely ensure our immediate demise. But whatever. I'm trying to go with the flow here.

"You don't have to sit with me," I tell Avi as he hesitates at my side. He's probably desperate to get away from me and go to his girlfriend. While he was super nice to me when we were alone, it was obviously out of duty. Now that Liron is in sight, he's surely waiting for me to let him off the hook. "You should talk to Liron," I say. "There's an empty spot next to her. She's probably saving it for you."

He looks surprised, but he nods his head and shrugs. "You sure?"

"Yep. I'll be fine. Go." Ugh. My stomach is tied in knots as he walks away from me. I wish I hadn't pushed him to go to her, but it's better than asking him to sit with me and have him reject me … or worse, have him sit next to me but long to be with Liron.

I find a spot next to Tori.

"You look like crap," she tells me.

"Thanks. I'm sure I couldn't have figured that out on my own."

"Your bangs look good, though, thanks to me. Although the only way to hide the nasty cuts on your chin would be to grow a beard. I don't think it'll be too hard for you."

I stand up. "If I wanted to be insulted, I would have sat next to Nathan. Nice talking to you. Bye."

"Wait!" she says, reaching out to grab the side of my pants. "I was just kidding."

"Do you even know how to be nice?"

I can see Tori perfectly in the light of the fire. Her blond hair shines like a halo, and her darker hair underneath looks like a protective shield. She looks up at me and says honestly, "I used to."

So now I feel sorry for her. Her little sincere comments make her vulnerable, which is something we have in common. I sit back down and stare into the fire.

"My parents thought I'd get over my anger about their divorce if I spent time with kids my own age and my own religion." She shakes her head in disgust. "Parents have no clue what their kids need."

Ha. "You think that's bad? I came on this trip to spend time with Avi. Look where that's gotten me." I gesture to Avi, sitting next to Liron.

"You think that's bad? My dad has a new girlfriend," Tori blurts out. "He says he wasn't dating her before they got divorced, but I'm not stupid."

"That's nothing. My mom dated a new guy every month before my stepfather. She totally had dating ADD. Then she got married and pregnant all in a year. I'm afraid she'll get parent ADD and not want the kid ... or Marc."

"As long as we're playing *Whose Life Sucks More?*, I can one-up you yet again. My parents just got divorced and my dad already cancels the weekends he's supposed to have me. My mom hopes he moves away and never comes back so she doesn't have to deal with him. But that's not what I want. I just wish … I just wish things could go back to the way they were."

I gaze longingly at Avi. "I do, too." I sigh, resigned to living in the real world.

Jess groans as she sits down next to us.

"Where have you been, Cleo?" I ask my best friend.

"Cleo? Wait, what happened to your chin? Did George the Zit spread?"

"No. While you were being carried like Cleopatra on the stretcher, the real wounded—me—finished the run bandaged up like Frankenstein."

"Yeah, well *I* just puked my guts out. Did you ever realize how much vertigo you can get lying on a stretcher bouncing up and down like a frickin' basketball? I had a death grip on the sides the entire time. I seriously thought I was gonna bounce right off."

Miranda, who I just notice is sitting on the other side of Tori, leans forward. "I'm sick of hearing you guys be all negative. I want each of you to say something positive."

Positive? I point to my gauzed-up forearms, gesture to my bloody chin and then to Avi talking to Liron, and then, as the cherry on top of my miserable life, I lift up my bangs to show off George the Zit.

"Say something, Amy," Miranda insists. "Something positive. I'm sure it'll make you feel better."

"Okay, Miranda. I've got it." I motion the girls to lean in close to hear my positive words. "At least I'm not dead."

How's that for positivity?

I have to admit it does make me feel better.

19

Physical strength is needed for obstacle courses,
but mental strength is needed when being close
to your ex-boyfriend.

Tori plops herself down on my cot during a fifteen-minute break the next day. "I hear we're sleeping in the desert at some point."

"Why would we do that when we live in such luxury right here?" I gesture at the bulging springs above me.

"Maybe they want to toughen us up."

"Oh, please. I'm tough enough. Any tougher and I'll grow balls and a hairy chest."

As if the thought of sleeping in the desert at night isn't scary enough, Ronit is leading us to the activity Avi warned me about.

Shooting an M16 rifle.

So now we're all standing in line, waiting to be issued a big rifle.

"I'm afraid of guns," I say, but nobody seems to be listening to me. They're all too excited. I guess it wouldn't hurt to hold the thing.

I have to sign for it and check that the serial number of the issued weapon, written next to my name, matches the actual number on the rifle. I can almost feel testicles growing between my legs as it's handed to me (I'm kidding, of course … about the testicles growing between my legs, not about being handed my very own weapon).

"Do you have any colors besides black?" I ask the guy handing out the guns.

"Are you kidding?"

"Of course I'm kidding. Although I wouldn't mind a pink one to match my luggage." The guy shakes his head and I think he mumbles something like *American princess,* but I can't be sure.

You should see the American boys in our unit as they're given their weapons. By the GI Joe expressions on their faces, you'd think they were just handed a Man Badge.

"I'll show you mine if you show me yours," Nathan jokes when we're standing under a canopy at the range, waiting for further instructions.

"Don't annoy me, Nathan. I have a gun." Of course it's big and bulky and warm from the summer sun. I sling it over my shoulder, feeling every bit of a soldier now. I definitely look the part.

"It's not loaded," Nathan responds dryly.

After handing us safety goggles and earmuffs, Sergeant B-S brings out a big box full of metal "magazines" and shows us how to insert the empty magazine into the bottom of the rifle. We've learned about the parts of the M16 and the different types of bullets in the classroom. Weapons safety has been drilled into my head.

Rules of gun safety in a non-combat environment:

1. Never point the weapon at a person, and always point it in a safe direction
2. Don't put your finger on the trigger until you're ready to shoot the weapon
3. Keep the weapon unloaded until you're ready to use it

After loading their magazines with bullets and shoving them into their weapons, Avi and Liron lie on their stomachs in front of canvas sandbags, with one leg straight and the other leg bent for support. With their rifles resting on the sandbags, they aim for the paper target in front of them and ... bang!

When they get up and we're ordered into position on the range for dry firing—shooting without bullets, that is—I raise my hand.

Nimrod comes over to help. "Amy, what's the problem?"

"I'm not sure I can do this. I'm not really a gun person."

He laughs. "That's a good joke. Hey, Gefen! Come here!"

Avi jogs over to us. "What's going on?"

"Amy here says she's not a *gun person.*"

"You'll be shooting a target, Amy. Not people," Avi says.

"Yeah, I get that, but … I'm afraid of the kickback, or sidekick or whatever you call it, and the noise. I have sensitive ears."

"It's called recoil." Nimrod rolls his eyes. "Gefen, you deal with your girlfriend."

"We're not dating anymore!" I call after Nimrod as he hurries off to help someone else.

Avi lifts the earmuffs off my ears. "No need to shout. Can we be friends today?"

"Sure," I say, putting the earmuffs back in place. *"Friends."*

Avi crouches. "Lie down."

I lie on the ground and rest the rifle on the sandbag. Avi checks the weapon, making sure the bullet chamber thingy is empty.

"There's no recoil in dry firing," he assures me. "Now move the lever from *safe* to *semi.* Make sure it's never on *auto* or you'll empty that magazine with one trigger pull."

I move the toggle to *semi.* Then I double and triple check it to make sure I didn't accidentally move it to *auto.* That would not be fun.

"Now settle the hand guard of the weapon into the V between your thumb and forefinger on your non-firing hand." He gently takes my knee and slides it up so it's bent. "Bending one knee gives you more support. Aim at your target through the sight guide. When you're ready, put your finger on the trigger."

"Avi?"

"Yeah?"

I look up at him. "I'm embarrassed to say this, because I really am against killing and guns. But I'm kind of getting a rush from this. I feel powerful with a gun this big in my hands."

"Wait to say that until after you sleep with it tonight."

"Huh?"

"Soldiers sleep with their gun every night they're on base or on duty. Come on, stop stalling. Aim at your target, control your breathing, and squeeze the trigger after you exhale."

I look through the sight thingy, aim at my paper target, and pull the trigger.

"Good. Do it again."

I keep dry firing until Sergeant B-S comes around and tells us all to put the rifles on *safe* mode.

We're told to fill our magazines with ten bullets and push the magazine into the rifle. "When you're ready, switch to the *semi* position and fire one at a time until your magazine is empty," Sergeant B-S instructs us.

I get back in position and line up the sights with my target, but I'm too nervous to shoot. I hear everyone else firing their guns on either side of me. Listen, disasters happen to me wherever I go, and I can't keep random thoughts from running through my head. What if the M16 misfires? What if the shell of the bullet hits me when it's ejected and burns my scalp as it lands on my head? What if the recoil dislocates my shoulder?

"I can tell you're thinking too much," Avi says, appearing beside me again.

He lies on the ground, his body next to mine. I have to remind myself not to think about Avi and focus on the gun.

"I'm afraid of the *recoil*."

"You're lying down, so you won't feel so much of it. Line up your target," he tells me.

I line up the paper that seems way too far away for me to hit with a bullet less than the width of my pinky finger. "Done."

He places his fingers over mine. They're strong and soft and I wish my body wouldn't tingle with excitement from him being near me. I'm so afraid that I'll never be able to fully get over him.

"Ready?"

I squeeze my eyes shut and control my breathing. Unfortunately, my pulse is racing. But that's because Avi's body is pressed up against mine. His strong hands on mine remind me of the times he touched me intimately. I try and put those thoughts out of my mind as I say, "Ready."

"Exhale. Hold it…" His finger presses on mine and the rifle fires. The recoil definitely pushes my shoulder back, but not as hard or as bad as I feared.

"You okay?"

I pick up my head, now just a few inches away from Avi's. "Oh. My. God. That was *awesome*!"

"Just a few minutes ago you said you weren't a gun person."

"I'm not. You know, when they're used for aggression or war. But just shooting a target is so cool."

Avi scratches his temple as if he isn't quite sure how to say what he's about to say. "Umm ... I hate to break the news to you, but you didn't actually hit *your* target. You hit Jessica's. Her bullet went left of her target and ended up in the haystacks."

I lean back and watch as Jessica brags about hitting her target. She analyzes her precision with the range binoculars as if she's a sharpshooter.

"Oh. Maybe this time I shouldn't shut my eyes when I pull the trigger."

"That'd probably help your aim." I can see him trying to hide his laugh with a cough.

Avi watches as I aim again. I control my breathing and shoot.

"Did I hit it?"

He smiles at me. "No. It went low. You overcompensated for the recoil too much by lowering the barrel. Try again."

I keep firing until my magazine is empty. I hit the target a bunch of times. I still think guns are dangerous and scary. But in a controlled environment like this, it's not so bad.

After we shoot two more magazines full of live ammunition, and I've finally learned to hit the target consistently, we're taught how to clean and care for our weapon. Because we're just trainees and not real, full-time Israeli soldiers, we have to hand in our magazines. Unless we're on the range, our issued rifles won't be anywhere near live ammo.

"Keep your rifle in your possession at all times unless instructed otherwise," Ronit tells us. "And watch your weapon closely. Liron or I might sneak up on you and take it in the middle of the night. If you don't wake up and we end up with your weapon, you'll have to do pushups come morning. Whether you keep it under your pillow or next to you in bed is up to you."

I grip my M16. I feel the smooth barrel and ridged handgrip. Not my first choice in sleeping partners, that's for sure. But since I have to sleep with it, I might as well give it a name.

George II.

"You shoot that rifle like a warrior woman, Amy," Nathan says. "I think Avi has rubbed off on you."

I don't feel like a warrior woman in the evening, after showers and I'm sitting on my bed wondering how I'm going to sleep with George II. The cold, hard black metal with traces of grease doesn't match my pink pillow.

Checking out how the other girls are sleeping with their guns, I notice most of them are placing them under their pillows. If I want a crick in my neck in the morning, putting the rifle under my pillow would be a great idea.

I don't want a sore neck in the morning.

Since I slide my arm under my pillow to sleep every night (it's hereditary; my dad does it, too), I figure George II will be better off if I sleep hugging him. I pull the covers up and lie on my pillow. Pulling George II closer, I hug him tight.

If Avi could see me now, hugging a black rifle tight enough so that Liron or Ronit can't steal it away from me in the middle of the night, he'd probably be proud.

I just wish it was Avi I was hugging instead of a big piece of metal. If only I could hug Avi tight enough so no girl could steal him away from me, I'd be happy.

Unfortunately, life doesn't work that way.

20

When your mom told you life isn't fair,
she wasn't kidding.

The next day we're off to the obstacle course again. Avi isn't with us, so we're without a team leader. Liron said Sergeant B-S called him into his office, and nobody has seen him since.

Determined to master the monkey bars, I take a deep breath when it's my turn and swing my body from one bar to the next. My team cheers me on ... even Tori, who has lost a tiny bit of her edge. We've fallen behind because of me, but when I finish the monkey bars without help and everyone claps for me, I catch a genuine smile on Tori's face as she congratulates me.

We still lose the race to Liron's team, but not by much. I think our team has finally become a cohesive unit, bolstered and strengthened by each other. When we all give high fives to each other, I catch sight of Avi standing next to Sergeant B-S. They both have very serious expressions on their faces.

Avi tells us we did a good job, then pulls me aside.

"If you're gonna tell me I should have gone up that rope by myself, I just couldn't," I tell him. "Next time I'll try. I promise."

"It's not about the rope, Amy."

He's definitely concerned about something. "What's wrong?"

"It's your *safta*."

My grandma? I swallow hard, thinking the worst. She has cancer, but I thought she was doing okay. Was I wrong? "Is...is she okay?" I hardly get the words out because there's a lump in my throat.

"Your father called. She was taken to the hospital last night and he thinks you should go there. Just in case."

"Just in case of *what*?"

He shrugs. "I don't know."

"What *exactly* did he say?"

"Sergeant Ben-Shimon gave me a forty-eight hour leave and use of a car. Come on, we can talk about it on the way."

I say my goodbyes to everyone in my unit. Even though Avi and I are abandoning them, Sergeant B-S says he'll take over as team leader for the next forty-eight hours until Avi comes back. My farewell is filled with tears, because I'm not coming back. And while I hated being here, I loved it too.

It takes me less than a half hour to pack up. Avi accompanies me to the *bittan* and doesn't leave my side the entire time. In the car, we're finally alone—without military restrictions or rules.

"So what did my dad say?" I ask.

"He said not to panic until they know more. He just wanted you with the family in case it's something serious."

"What if she's dying?"

"Don't start thinking the worst."

"That's like telling my dog Mutt not to smell crotches."

He looks sideways at me as he drives. "Is that why you think the worst of me?"

"You kissed Liron *more than once*. I didn't make it up."

"I admitted to kissing Liron. When you kissed Nathan, I heard you out and we got past it. Why won't you hear me out?"

I might as well tell him the truth. "Because I'm afraid."

"Of the truth?"

Of course. The truth hurts most of the time. I have a history of pushing people away in an effort to avoid the truth. "Yeah," I tell him. "I'm afraid of the truth. I think of you being attracted to someone else, and I feel sick. And when I visualize you kissing someone else, the pain is just too great. I thought you, of all people, would never disappoint me."

I look out the window, trying to avoid looking right at Avi. Admitting how much his betrayal has affected me makes me vulnerable.

"I've been waiting for some hint that you want to fight for us."

"I'm done fighting," I say.

"I'm not."

"It's an occupational hazard for you. You're a soldier, trained to fight."

"So what do you want, Amy? You want to be enemies? Friends?"

"Friends sounds good. You know, what we are without the dating part. That way, I have no expectations." Maybe Noah has it right . . . no expectations means you don't get hurt.

Avi takes a deep breath. "If just being friends is what you want, I'll give you that. But when you're ready to fight for more, let me know. Because nothing is as intense as when we're together. Admit it."

"I admit it. But who says intense is best?"

"Me. And you, if you'd just open your eyes long enough to realize we might not be the most perfect couple, but we're better together than apart. Truth is, I'm afraid of losing you," he blurts out. "I know this probably isn't the best time to bring it up, but we don't have many chances to be alone. Nathan isn't the one—you know that. Sure, he talks a lot. Each word out of me is a struggle sometimes. But you and I . . . Amy . . ." He hesitates, and I can just feel him trying to get the right words out to express his feelings. For a guy who hardly ever talks in public, expressing emotion out loud is harder than shooting a flea a hundred meters away. "We're just *right*."

The problem is, I don't think my heart can handle another Avi breakup. I'm programmed to be emotional; I can't help it. For better or worse, my attitude and "drama queen-ness" defines who I am. Avi, on the other hand, is emotionally and drama-challenged. And although I came on this boot camp program in order to see him, maybe it was God's way of hinting that we're just too different.

"I'm always going to be afraid a smarter girl or a prettier girl is going to lure you away from me. Listen, I don't blame you for being attracted to Liron. She's beautiful, she can scale walls, climb ropes, and she carries a rifle. If I liked girls, I'd go for her too."

"Just hear me out, okay?"

My resolve is weakening fast. I have the childish urge to cover my ears with my palms and sing *la, la, la, la, la, la* so I don't hear what happened between Avi and Liron. But I guess I can't hide from the truth forever.

"Okay, Avi. Tell me why you kissed Liron."

21

Sometimes the truth hurts...
but you can't let it consume your life.

Everyone can take lessons in life from the Israelis.

We're driving north toward Tiberias. Every time I look out the window, I see Israelis doing the same things we do back home. I see kids playing on playgrounds, teens playing soccer, and people eating at restaurants. I wonder why Israelis don't act like they're living in a war zone. How can they be so strong-willed? How can they know the truth —that some of the countries surrounding them would like nothing better than to destroy their country—and still live carefree lives?

I brace myself for the truth of what happened between Avi and Liron. Listen, I'm half Israeli myself. I can act like an Israeli and tackle any obstacle that comes my way. At least I think I can.

"Now probably isn't the best time to talk about it, with

your *safta* in the hospital, but we might not get another chance."

"At least it'll get my mind off of wondering what's wrong with her. Go ahead, Avi. I need to know."

"Survival training was a total mind game," he tells me. "Lack of sleep, being blindfolded and finding out what it was like to be captured by terrorists, watching actual footage of Jews being brutally murdered just because they were Jewish or Israeli. Some of the bodies were so mutilated you wondered if they were killed by humans or beasts. You question your faith in God, because why would He let those things happen? You end up puking your guts out. You get so sad that every guy, no matter how tough, breaks down and cries like a baby. Then anger and a craving for revenge replaces the sorrow. Fury seeps from every pore of your body. I was so exhausted there were times I had no clue if my thoughts were my own, and at times I was so enraged I wanted to rush out and kill every terrorist single-handedly."

I watch as he shakes his head and lets out a slow breath. I'm not sure if it's because it hurts to recall that week of training or if it's because he desperately wants his country to live in peace but doesn't see how that's possible. Either way, I'm stunned by the rush of words and emotion.

"Afterward, I needed you, Amy," he continues. "I needed you so damn bad. I wanted to hold you in my arms again, feel your warm sweet body against mine to remind me that there's something good out there, that this world isn't only full of hatred and evil. Liron felt the same way. Her boyfriend was stationed on another base and you were in the States. I remember what you said about it being okay if we saw other people. Being with Liron until I started feeling human again seemed like a great solution at the time." He gives a short, cynical laugh. "But it sucked, because she wasn't you." His swipes his eyes with the back of his hand, getting emotional. "She wasn't you," he chokes out.

I'm starting to cry now too. "It's not fair, Avi. We found each other but live in two different countries. Just when I feel the closest to you, we're ripped apart. It's not fair."

"Amy, tell me anyone else can make your heart pound like it does when you're with me," he says. "Tell me you think anything or anyone can compare with it, and I'll give up on us."

Oh, God. I want us to get back together, because nobody can make me feel like he does. I want him so bad. I can't deny it any longer, to myself or him.

"No, Avi. Don't give up on us." The Israeli side of me bursts forward with a vengeance, and I think my fighting spirit has finally come out. Boot camp has changed me. I put my hand over his. "I forgive you. I can't forget what you did with Liron just as much as you probably can't forget I kissed Nathan. But I can definitely forgive."

He lifts my hand to his lips and kisses it. We're both at peace with everything that happened, except there's one thing I probably should tell him. Making up feels so good and carefree. But… "Umm, Avi, I kind of lied to you back on base."

"About what?"

I clear my throat. As long as Avi told the truth, I might as well spill the beans. "Nathan and I have never been a couple. I kind of coerced him into pretending we were dating."

Avi winks at me. "I knew that."

22

Forgiveness takes a lot less energy than holding grudges.

Three hours after leaving boot camp, we reach the hospital. Avi takes my hand after we pass through hospital security and steers me down the front corridor. The closer I get to seeing *Safta*, the more scared I get. What if she looks different? What if she looks weaker than she did last year? I hate cancer. It's as dangerous and deadly as a terrorist.

Avi asks the lobby receptionist something in Hebrew. She points to the elevator bank. The inside of the Baruch Padeh Medical Center hospital in Tiberias looks just like hospitals back home, with stark white walls and the scent of purified air bursting through the air conditioning vents.

"You okay?" Avi asks as we're riding up the elevator.

"Yeah. Why?"

"Your nails are digging into my palm." He loosens my hand and shows me the nail indentations in his skin.

"Sorry. Truth is, I'm freaking out."

He puts his arm around me, holds me tight to him, and lightly kisses the top of my head. "I'm here for you. Always. You know that, even if you don't always want to believe it."

Whenever I've needed Avi for my minor but frequent emergencies in my life, he's been there for me. Whether it was on the base or on the phone or in person, he's always around when I'm desperate for someone to keep my spirits high and lift me up ... even physically.

He slows his pace when we get closer to the room. "Remember, it's okay to cry." He shrugs when I glance up at him. "My mom told me that after my brother died."

"And *did* you cry, Avi?"

He bites his bottom lip and nods. "Yeah ... I did." He clears his throat and lifts his head high. "Come on," he says, nudging me forward into the room.

I take a deep breath and peek my head inside. *Safta* has an oxygen mask over her nose and mouth. Her eyes are closed and it looks like she's sleeping peacefully in the hospital bed, her pale complexion making her look like an angel. My dad is sitting next to the bed. He rushes from the chair and opens his arms to hug me, but when he takes a closer look his eyes go wide with shock.

"Amy. *Mah carah*? What happened to you?" He gestures to my arms and chin as he inspects my scratched face.

"Oh, that. Umm … I kinda fell on rocks. Well, I guess *skidded* is more like it."

"You look like you've been in battle."

"That's kind of how I felt. But it's better today. I've turned into a warrior woman." Sort of.

Back when I begged my dad to let me go on this trip, he warned me not to complain no matter how hard boot camp turned out to be. Either I could stay at my aunt and uncle's house with him on the *moshav* all summer (with possibly no chance of seeing Avi), or I could go on the army portion of the *Sababa* trip with my friends (and possibly see Avi). But if I chose boot camp, I'd better suck it up.

I'd like you to know that this is me sucking it up. Pre-army Amy would definitely be whining *Aba, they make us get up before the sun is up, and run in the dark, and pee and poop in stinky holes, and sleep with our guns, and eat jam with bees in it, and do boy pushups, and march in straight lines, and scale walls, and sleep in beds with springs missing above our heads, and dig holes with big, hairy spiders in them …*

… but I don't.

"Is *Safta* going to be okay?" I ask, because that's the only concern that I have at this moment. I can't lose my only living grandparent. God *can't* let that happen.

Although what really scares me is that God *can* let that happen. Rabbi Glassman says that death is a part of life. We don't have a choice to live, and we don't have a choice as to when we'll naturally die.

"They'll be taking her for a CAT scan in the morning. We'll know more after the scan and when we get the results of her blood test. When she woke up she was in pain and disoriented, so they gave her a sedative. I don't expect her to wake up until the morning, so you might as well go back to the *moshav* and get some rest." He inspects me again. "Wait, you look different, and it's not just the scratches. Did you get a *haircut* on the base?"

"Yeah. It's a long story; don't ask."

"Okay, I won't." He knows better than to ask for details, because he's well aware of my special ability to get into trouble wherever I go. He shakes hands with Avi. "Thanks for bringing Amy here."

"*Ayn b'yah*—no problem. They gave me a forty-eight-hour leave."

I stand next to my *safta*, bow my head, and pray silently to God to take care of her—just in case He's listening and just in case He wants to answer my prayer.

I don't know what I'll do if I lose her. I didn't even know I had a grandmother until a year ago, and now here she is in a hospital. I feel like she's slipping away from my life already. She never let me tell her how much she's helped me spiritually. During my Jewish conversion classes, whenever I thought about the Jewish matriarchs, I always imagined they would look and act exactly like my *safta*. I read that Abraham's wife Sarah gave birth at the age of ninety and died at the ripe old age of 127. I wish my *safta* could be like Sarah (obviously not the giving birth at ninety part ... just the living until 127 part).

"Amy, I'm gonna step out so you and your *aba* can talk alone. I'll be right outside the door if you need me," Avi says.

My dad stands beside me and strokes my back as we both look down at the sweetest woman I've ever known. "I came home from school when I was six and told her an eight-year-old named Ido had pushed me," he tells me. "Can you guess what she did?"

"Went to school and threatened Ido if he didn't leave you alone?"

"No."

"Called Ido's mother and told her that her kid was a bully?"

"No. She told me to handle it myself. She said I'd have to deal with bullies all my life—so I might as well figure out how to deal with them at the age of six."

I try to picture my grandma as a young woman, strong and full of energy.

"Did you know she was in a war?" my dad asks me.

"What war?" I know all Israelis have to serve in the military. The country has been through their share of wars since they were recognized by the UN in 1948, but I can't imagine my grandmother wearing an army uniform or carrying a gun.

"She was in the Sinai War of '56. You should ask her about it. They wouldn't let women on the front lines back then, so she dressed as a boy."

"Whoa. I can't believe my grandmother was in a war.

I can't wait to tell Roxanne back at school, who brags that her great-grandmother was one of the first women pilots." *Pilot, shmilot.* My grandmother was on the *front lines.* I guess I'm not the only kick-ass warrior woman in the family. "So what happened with you and Ido? Did you tell him to stop pushing you?"

"Oh, I told him. Right after that, he pushed me again."

"What'd you do?"

"Well, the next day I came to school with a gift for Ido."

"Like a fist-in-your-face kind of gift?"

"No. Like a new basketball my aunt gave me after she visited the States."

Let me get this straight. "Ido pushed you, and you gave him a gift?"

"Since my mom wouldn't intervene, and there was no way I could fight a big kid two years older than me, I figured trying to be friends with him was my best option."

"So you became friends with the bully?"

He nods.

"That's a sellout. You shouldn't have to give the bully something. That's just *wrong* on so many levels."

"I had to sacrifice a little in order to get what I wanted. We ended up being friends."

I guess we all sacrifice at some time or another. I just hate having to do it so often.

"*Aba,* is she going to die?"

"Eventually."

"You know what I mean. Is this *it*? Is this the start of the end?"

"She had her final chemo treatment last week. They suspect her white blood cell count is low."

"But what if it's more than that?" I cry.

He puts his arm around me. "Let's not worry about that until the morning, when we know more. Let Avi take you back to the *moshav*."

"I don't want to leave *Safta*," I say, watching the oxygen mask fog up when she exhales.

"I know. But you can't do anything for her tonight. You can come back as soon as you wake up in the morning. Now go."

I hug him tight, wondering how I could have ever been distant from my father. I'm so grateful God brought him back into my life. I don't know what I'd do without him, especially now, with my mom and Marc starting a new family.

I don't know if I'll fit in. Will they still have time for me *and* a new baby? But one look at my dad and I know he'll never be out of my life again, no matter if I try to push him away or not. (Believe me, I've tried it. Especially when Avi was in town and my dad was grilling him, having the "Don't Do It" sex talk with both of us multiple times, and acting as an overprotective chaperone the entire time.)

After taking me for a quick dinner, Avi parks the car in front of my aunt and uncle's house on the *moshav*. It's on top of a big mountain overlooking the Kineret lake.

It's rustic and dusty and total farmland, but it feels like home.

Poor Avi had to listen to me cry and sniff and blow my nose every two seconds all the way from the hospital, although he didn't seem to mind. He held my hand the entire time (except when I was being gross and blowing my nose, and when we stopped for dinner). Seriously, just having him here with me gives me strength.

Avi lives a few houses down on the opposite side of the very narrow gravel road, but he doesn't just drop me off.

My cousin Osnat (pronounced O'snot – and yes, it's a very popular Israeli name) is the first person to see me. She's sitting on the sofa, watching television with my aunt (*Doda* Yucky), my Uncle Chaim (I call him Uncle Chime, because I can't do that back-throat-noise Hebrew-pronunciation thing), and my little toddler cousin Matan (who is not naked, for once).

They all wrap me and Avi in big hugs. Even Osnat, and she's not the most warm and fuzzy person I've ever met—although we definitely get along way better now than we used to. I can tell she's been crying, too, because her eyes are all bloodshot.

"Amy, what happened to your chin? And your arms?" *Doda* Yucky looks at Avi accusingly.

He holds his hands up. "Don't look at me. She managed to do that all on her own."

"You beat yourself up?" Osnat says. "In the morning you'll have to tell us how you managed to do that."

I know she's just joking. Normally I'd have some witty comeback, but I'm too upset and exhausted to think of one.

"Are you hungry?" *Doda* Yucky asks. "Let me fix you both something. You've had such a long day."

"I took her to Marinado by Kibbutz Ein Gev," Avi tells them. "I couldn't resist stopping there for one of their burgers."

I sit with my aunt, uncle, and cousins in their small living room as we catch up on the past year. Even though we talk every week, it's not the same as actually spending time with them. Uncle Chime laughs when I tell him about my experiences on the army base, and even tells me a funny story about digging ditches when he was in the army. I guess digging ditches is a rite of passage for Israeli soldiers. *Doda* Yucky shares her own stories about being an instructor on one of the bases. Matan climbs on her lap and dangles off her knees while she's talking. *Doda* Yucky has always been sweet to me. She never stops smiling, and she loves everyone she comes in contact with.

Then the conversation turns to *Safta's* health. *Doda* Yucky tells me how she found her unconscious. The somber mood returns as they tell me to pray for the best.

A yawn escapes my mouth.

"You need sleep," Uncle Chime tells me. "You look exhausted."

"I am." Although I don't know if I *can* sleep. Too many thoughts are running through my head, but I'm so overtired, hopefully my eyes will close as soon as I hit my pillow.

After Avi helps bring my suitcases in from the car, Osnat drags her pillow and blanket out of her room. "Amy can sleep in my room. I'll sleep in *Safta's* room tonight," she says.

I peer inside Osnat's room. Just like I remembered, it has two twin beds situated across the room from each other. "I don't want to kick you out of your room. You've got two beds. We can share."

"It's not a problem. Really. I'd rather sleep in *Safta's* bed. I'd feel closer to her somehow. Besides, you snore."

I give a huff. "That's *so* not true."

"You're asleep, so how would you know? Seriously, last summer I needed earplugs when you slept in my room."

I look up at Avi. "I do *not* snore."

"I believe you," he says. "But right now I need to go across the street to let my parents know I'm here."

My heart starts racing in panic. I grab a fistful of his shirt and hold on tight. "But you're coming back tonight, right?"

"If you want me to."

"I don't want you to leave for a second."

"You need to get ready for bed, Amy. I can't exactly be with you then, unless you want your uncle and dad to threaten to give me a second circumcision." He kisses me lightly on the lips. "Take a hot shower and enjoy it. You haven't had one in a while. I'll be back after I say hi to my parents and wash up. I promise."

Famous last words.

I stand in the foyer pouting like my dog Mutt when he watches me put my jacket on. If I *was* a real dog, I would whimper just like Mutt, too. But I'm not a dog and I have to suck it up and stay positive.

I can do positive.

Taking a deep breath, I grab my PJs and head for the one bathroom. There's still an open keyhole/peephole in the door for anyone inclined to look at someone peeing or taking a dump. I undress quickly, unwrap the gauze from my arms, and turn the water on, hoping none of my Israeli family members open the door without knocking.

When the water turns hot, it's like the Almighty Lord has sent a miracle down to earth just for me. Being super gentle while soaping the still-raw cuts on my arms, I lather up, scrub, rinse, and repeat a few times before letting the water just run down my body. Ahh, this feels great.

I hear the door open.

"Helloooo, I'm in here," I say loudly, then stick my head out of the curtain to see who's barged in on me.

It's little Matan, with his corkscrew hair and Power Ranger pajamas on. "*Shalom*, Ami," he says, smiling wide. He says my name Ah-mee instead of Amy.

"*Shalom*. Do you mind? I'm in the shower here." I know the kid doesn't understand English, but you'd think he'd get the hint. No such luck.

My little toddler cousin pulls down his pants and starts peeing in the toilet next to the shower. Does he not care that I'm in here, totally naked behind the curtain? To top it off, he starts scratching his butt while he's peeing. Eww. Please don't tell me every guy does this.

When he's done, he gives his thingie a little shake, pulls up his pants, and waves to me with a big happy-go-lucky smile on his face. I'll never get over the fact that guys don't wipe their wee-wees after they pee. It just seems so *unsanitary*. It also seems unsanitary that Matan is going out of the bathroom without washing his hands. Totally *not* acceptable.

"Yo, Matan!" I call after him.

"*Ken?*" Yes?

I'm still naked, in the shower with shampoo in my hair and soap running down my body, with my head the only thing peeking out from the curtain. "Wash your hands, little buddy."

"*Lo meda'bear Angleet*, Ami." He doesn't understand English, and he's waiting for me to translate what I just said.

How the hell am I supposed to know what *wash your germy hands* is in Hebrew? I let go of the curtain and rub my hands together using the universal hand-washing motion, then point to the sink. "Wash your hands," I tell him again, hoping he understands this time.

Matan points to my now exposed boobs and says, "*Tzee-tzeem g'doleem!*"

I know that *gadol* means "big," and I can just imagine that *tzee-tzeem* means "boobs" by the direction of his pointing finger. Would he think it polite of me to point to his wee-wee and announce *"Pee-pee katan!"*—Hebrew for his ding-a-ling is tiny?

I quickly pull the shower curtain back over my body. Keeping one hand on the curtain, I point to the sink again. "Wash, Matan, or I swear I'm telling your mom you don't clean your hands after peeing." Yes, I'm aware he doesn't know what my threat means, but it makes me feel better saying it.

Doda Yucky knocks on the door. "Amy, is Matan in there?"

"Yep. He sure is."

She opens the door, apologizes, and helps him quickly wash his hands before shooing him out. "I'm so sorry. I'll make sure he doesn't do that again."

Matan points in the general direction of my boob area hiding behind the curtain and says to his mother, *"L'Amy yesh tzee-tzeem g'doleem!"*

Doda Yucky looks embarrassed as she says, "He doesn't mean anything by that."

"Uh huh." I'll just file that into the folder of embarrassing/humiliating moments in my life.

After my shower, I change into PJs and feel like a new person. At least a new person with scratched-up arms and a chin with racer marks on it.

"Is Avi back yet?" I ask Osnat. She's sitting on our *safta's* bed, looking at a photo album.

"No." Osnat, who's my age and will be in the Israeli army in a year, looks vulnerable and lost. *"Safta* always looked forward to your Saturday calls, you know."

"She never seemed tired of hearing about what was going on in my life." There aren't many people who like to hear the sound of your voice and are happy to listen to you, no matter what you're saying. *Safta* is one of those people. Some kids hate talking to their elderly grandparents on the phone, but I can't wait until I wake up Saturday morning and can call my family in Israel.

"Here's a picture of us when we went to the *Kotel*, the Western Wall," she tells me. I move closer and look at the picture. It shows my aunt, my uncle, *Safta*, and my two cousins pushing tiny pieces of paper into the cracks in the Wall.

I've read about the Wall, the only standing structure from the ancient Jewish Temple. It's also called the Wailing Wall because Jews mourn the destruction of the Temple and grieve while praying there. "What are you doing in this picture?" I ask her.

"Putting prayers into the cracks. It's customary to do that. People think God is closer there than other places, and will answer your prayers."

Oh, great. Why hadn't I known this sooner? I definitely think a trip to the Western Wall is in order. The only problem is that it's in Jerusalem, a few hours from the *moshav.* In another picture, Matan is kissing the Wall while standing next to *Safta*.

I sit on the edge of *Safta's* bed, thinking how lucky Osnat is. Our grandma has lived with her since she was born. I know some teens would hate sharing their home with their grandparent, but I would have loved it. Especially *my* grandma, because she's sweet and kind and has definitely given me good advice *when I asked for it* (unlike my mother, who's a master at giving me unsolicited opinions, suggestions, and critiques).

"What is *Safta* really like?"

Osnat looks up and smiles. "Seriously, with *Safta* what you see is it. When I was younger we used to go out in the middle of the night when we both couldn't sleep and we'd sit on the edge of the mountain and talk... about nothing and everything."

"That's so cool."

"It was. And there's this area about a mile away where eagles fly over a ravine. We'd sit there for hours, talking about Israel and freedom and history." She wipes tears away. "I guess you kinda missed out by living in America. I always think you have it so easy, and I guess I get jealous of your material stuff." Osnat closes the album and sits up. "What's with you and Avi?"

"What's with you and O'dead?" I ask her, quickly changing the subject to her boyfriend. Israelis are not overly gushy or lovey-dovey types, and I'm afraid she'll make fun of me if I open up and really tell her how I feel about Avi. "Are you guys still dating?"

"O'dead and I broke up. He's dating Ofra."

"Wait. Isn't Ofra dating Doo-Doo?"

"She dumped him."

Wait a minute. "Your best friend stole your boyfriend?"

"Kind of. But I'm over it."

I guess when Jessica started dating Mitch, Mitch and I were still technically a couple even though I'd already met Avi.

Teenage dating is definitely complicated. Before Avi and I met, my friends and I used to joke that marrying your high school sweetheart was an urban myth. No teen relationships I know of have lasted.

"You never answered about you and Avi."

"We had some issues. But everything's great now."

"Really?"

I think about Avi, and how I can't imagine him out of my life. I'm glad I decided to give us another chance, because I don't want to be an urban myth. I want us to be real. And being real means dealing with real issues (and drama, because my name is Amy Nelson-Barak and I can't avoid it).

I stand by the doorway to see if Avi is in the hallway. Nobody on the *moshav* locks their doors. Everyone is like family, so they just walk into each other's houses as if they live there. I can't imagine me just prancing into Mr. Obermeyer's condo in our building without knocking. If he owned a gun, he'd shoot first and ask questions later.

"*Shalom*! Earth to Amy." I look over at my cousin, who's waving her hand at me. "Are you daydreaming about Avi again? Listen, since I'm not dating anyone, maybe next summer before my military service I'll come visit you in America to meet American boys. I'm sick of Israeli guys."

I hear the front door open and my heart leaps when I see Avi. He's wearing black sweats and a T-shirt. When he smiles at me, a warm calmness spreads over my body. I think God definitely had something to do with bringing us together. Life *is* too short not to be with the person you love the most, even if you have to work through both of your emotional baggage while you're together. Who better to deal with your issues than a person who loves you?

"Hey," he says. "You okay?"

"I am now that you're here," I answer back as I hug his waist and bury my head into his chest.

Osnat pretends to gag. "Ugh, please get out of here before I catch whatever love disease you have."

"Come on," I say, leading Avi to Osnat's room.

He watches from the guest bed while I blow-dry my hair. Afterward, I sit next to him while he takes the extra gauze the nurse on the base gave me and carefully rewraps my forearms.

"I hope one day I can take care of you," I tell him.

"You already do. You're a constant reminder that life is not one-dimensional. I forget that sometimes."

I lean my back against his chest and hold his arms around me. I feel so safe and protected wrapped in his arms.

"I've got to report back to the base in two days," he says quietly. "We might not get to see each other after that. I assume you're not going back to the base."

There's so much I want to tell him right here, right

now. I turn around and sit on my knees, facing him. "I need to say some stuff, Avi. And I need to say it before I lose my nerve, so don't interrupt me." I take a deep breath, hold his hands in mine, and look into the depths of his eyes. I can get lost in those chocolate depths so easily. "I admire you so much … the way you lead by example … the incredible drive you have to succeed at whatever you're doing … the way you know how to lead our group with authority, but you can also follow directions like you do with Sergeant Ben-Shimon … I admire the skills you possess in so many different areas … I love the way you protect the ones you love … I love the passion you have for your country and your willingness and dedication to protect it at all costs … "

I cup Avi's cheek in my hand. "I think God had something to do with us getting together, because we're so different. But I seriously think we were meant to be together."

He swipes away tears falling down my cheeks. "God definitely had something to do with it. Amy?"

"Yeah?"

"I think we can do it. You know, just date each other. Nobody else."

"You do?"

He nods.

"Me, too." One by one, my worries and fears and insecurities start melting away.

I lay my head in Avi's lap and he runs his fingers through my hair.

"I should leave," he says after a while.

I wrap my arms around him, holding tight. I know that if he leaves I'll be more of a mess than I already am. Avi makes me stronger. "No. Please don't go. Not yet." I look up at him, this boy/man who challenges me to be a better, stronger person. According to Liron's assessment, I've ruined his Israeli warrior reputation and he's still unconditionally by my side. I don't know if anyone else in this universe could handle me except a guy like Avi.

I hear the front door open. I'm too weak to sit up. My dad cracks the door to my room a minute later. "Amy, you up?"

"Yeah. Just so you know, Avi's with me."

"Oh." If it was any other time, my dad would order Avi out. And maybe even threaten his life. But he sees Avi comforting me and his face softens. "Just ... keep the door open. Okay? And no touching ... things ... things, um, things you're not supposed to be touching."

Yeah, that's how comfortable my dad is talking about sex. He stutters and hesitates and then asks me to talk to my mom. Unfortunately for him, my mom is back in the United States.

My dad is about to give us privacy when Avi calls out, "Ron?"

My dad stops and asks, *"Mah?"* which means "what" in Hebrew.

"Todah rabah." Thank you very much.

My dad's response is a nod.

Avi slides his body behind me on the bed and holds me tight the entire night. I think he stayed up all night. When I woke up and cried against his chest, he caressed my hair and wiped the tears from my face. When I whispered my fears about *Safta* dying an hour later, he listened, gave support, and rubbed my back until I fell back asleep. And when I open my eyes in the morning, he's watching me sleep.

"You must be exhausted," I say, my body curling into the warmth of his body heat. It feels so good in his arms, it almost lulls me back to sleep. But thoughts of *Safta* bring me back to reality.

After a quick breakfast, Avi drives me and my dad to the hospital a half hour away. My uncle and Osnat follow in their car. While my dad and Uncle Chime talk to the doctors and nurses about the next test to determine what's wrong with *Safta*, and Osnat goes to the cafeteria to get coffee, I sit next to *Safta's* bed. Avi leans against the window sill off to the side, giving me privacy.

My grandmother slowly opens her eyes. It takes her a minute to adjust to her surroundings, but when her eyes focus on me she has an apologetic look on her face. She pulls off the oxygen mask. "Amy, *motek*, what are you doing here? You're supposed to be at boot camp."

"I came to make sure you're okay. And to be with you."

"I don't want … you to see me like this. It's no fun in a hospital watching some tired old lady sleep."

"You're not just some old lady," I tell her while I give her a gentle hug. "You're my *safta*. How are you feeling?"

"Like an old lady." Her wrinkled, frail hand reaches out and fingers the tiny Jewish star diamond pendant around my neck. She gave it to me last summer during my visit. "I'm so happy you're wearing it."

"I wear it every day. It reminds me of you."

She smiles that sweet grandma smile that makes me feel like everything in my life will be okay. "Are you having a nice vacation?"

"Well, being on the army base hasn't been much of a vacation. Avi's my unit leader," I say, gesturing to Avi over by the window.

"Avi, come closer. I can't see you all the way over there," *Safta* says, waving him over. "My eyes aren't what they used to be."

Avi kisses my *safta* on the cheek. He's known her since he was born. Last night he told me she's like a second grandmother to him. "*Mah nishmah?*—How are you?"

"*Beseder*—I'm fine. I got a little dizzy. I wish my children wouldn't declare it a national emergency."

"*Ima,* stop talking nonsense," my dad interrupts her as he comes into the room. "You were unconscious when Yucky found you. Don't brush it off as if nothing happened."

She shoos my dad away. "Go eat something in the cafeteria, Ron, and leave me alone with the young teenagers here." My dad starts to protest, but gives up when she raises her eyebrows and makes another "go away" hand gesture.

Ooh, I can just imagine her staring at him with raised eyebrows when he was a kid. My dad is a total guys' guy —muscular, masculine, and full of testosterone. Knowing that his frail old mom can make him back off with a raised eyebrow and a hand gesture amuses me to no end.

Once my dad is out of sight, *Safta* turns to Avi. "Is my granddaughter a good soldier?"

Yeah, umm ... no need to let my sweet, old, sick grandmother know I suck at being a soldier. I mean, seriously, the woman dressed as a boy to fight on the front lines. Knowing that her own flesh and blood can't even scale a wall or aim a gun without having a few stray bullets hit other people's targets could *kill* her. I take *Safta's* hand and pat it. "Why don't we talk about something else?" Preferably a topic that doesn't have to do with what a spaz I really am.

"She's definitely challenging herself," Avi says to *Safta*. "Right, Amy?"

"I shot an M16," I say, but don't tell her I hit other people's targets more often than my own.

"I did the obstacle course," I continue, but don't tell her I had to be escorted up the rope and had to step on people's backs during my first attempt on the monkey bars.

"I even picked bees out of the jam when I had kitchen duty." I don't mention the whole bee/Nathan/tongue incident, either.

She fingers the bandages on my arms. "What happened to you?"

"Yeah, that. I went on a night run up a mountain. The mountain and I kinda got into a fight. The mountain won."

"That's not true," Avi tells her. "Amy won. She took a hard fall, but kept going."

I guess he's right. I'm still new at looking at things in a positive light.

Safta rubs her fingers over my fingernails, which are totally trashed from boot camp. "I'm so proud of you, Amy."

"Me, too," Avi adds.

"Avi needs to be back at the base tomorrow," I tell her. "He only got a forty-eight-hour leave."

"Aren't you still supposed to be there?"

"Yeah, but I'm not going back. I want to be here with you."

"For what?" my *safta* asks.

I don't want to say it. I can't talk about death with the person I'm afraid is dying. "For you. What if, you know, you're *really* sick?"

"I'm not going to die so quickly, *motek*—sweetheart. But even if I did, I'd die happier knowing you're doing what you're supposed to do—live—instead of watching an old lady die." *Safta*, who seemed so weak a second ago, points her small finger at me. Her face gets stern and spunky, and it's another glimpse into her life as a woman ready to fight for something she believes in. "You're Amy Nelson-Barak. Do you know what Barak means in Hebrew?"

I shake my head.

"It means 'lightning.' Amy, you're a true Barak, inside and out. You have a fighting spirit. No Barak is a quitter, you hear me? Now, make me proud and go back to finish boot camp … and be a Barak."

I think my *safta* can give Sergeant B-S a run for his money.

23

---

*Who knew the best times of your life
can come out of the worst situations?*

We stay at the hospital all day, waiting for test results. Her white blood cell counts were low, but rose as the day wore on. Tomorrow, her doctor plans to do full scans to make sure her cancer hasn't spread, but my dad assures me her life isn't in immediate danger.

After we get back to the *moshav* and *Doda* Yucky makes dinner for us, I make the final decision to go back and complete boot camp. Soon I'm saying my goodbyes to my family while Avi says his goodbyes to his. Before my own family has time to miss me, I'll have graduated boot camp and be back on the *moshav*. Avi's family isn't so lucky. After my *Sababa* group graduates, Avi and the rest of the Sayeret Tzefa trainees are going to intense training at the Counter

Terror School. The time with the *Sababa* group was supposed to be a relaxing break for them between parachuting and Counter Terror School. Unfortunately for Avi, I don't think being with my unit has been relaxing.

"Be good," my dad says, bending down into the passenger side window to hug me as Avi climbs behind the wheel. "Avi, keep her safe."

"I will."

I know it's going to be a long drive, because the base is south of the Dead Sea. The sun is setting when we reach Haifa, and we still have more than a few hours to go.

I talk to Avi about Miranda liking Nathan, but Nathan liking Tori … and Tori not liking anyone. When I ask about Noah, Avi tells me that he's a good guy who really doesn't mind doing any of the jobs the army assigns him.

"I've never seen Noah upset. Not even once," he tells me.

"When I first met Noah, I thought he'd be a good match for Miranda," I say. "Or maybe Nimrod would."

"Miranda isn't Nimrod's type."

I tsk. "What's that supposed to mean? Just because she has a little extra padding doesn't mean—"

"Nimrod's gay."

"Gay? As in … "

"He's got a boyfriend."

"Does he know that *you* know?"

"Everyone knows. He doesn't exactly keep it a secret. This is Israel. While we might not be the most tolerant people in the world, being gay here isn't a big deal. Even in the military. Nimrod's a damn good soldier, and we're lucky he's on our squad. He's practically fearless and makes me a better soldier."

"*You* make *me* a better soldier, Avi," I tell him. "I just wish I was a better friend to Miranda. I want her to be happy. Do you think setting her up with Noah would work?"

Avi takes my hand in his and kisses my palm. "Trying to make the world perfect again?"

"I'm good at doing it for other people. I seem to screw up my own life pretty good most of the time. I guess we all have our talents, don't we?"

He nods.

"Speaking of making life perfect, Avi. Umm…do you remember last summer when we pulled off to the side of the road?"

"Yeah. How could I forget?"

"Okay, so I know I'm a girl and shouldn't be asking this, but you only live once and life is short. Can we pull off the road? We're in the middle of a deserted road in the middle of nowhere, Israel."

Avi flashes me a shocked expression. "I thought you didn't want to have sex until we were married."

"I'm not talking about sex. I'm talking about kissing, and maybe a little body exploration…" But as my voice trails off, I wonder what Avi has in mind. "Why? Do *you* want to have sex?"

He nods. "I'm a guy, Amy. Of course I want to have sex with my girlfriend."

"You do?"

"Oh, yeah," he says, his voice deep and sexy.

My eyes graze over him, and now I know why being alone together brings us closer to dangerous territory. These are the times my dad and mom have warned me about, when my commitment to staying a virgin until I'm married is compromised by my raging teenage hormones.

"Don't look at me like that, Amy."

"Like what?"

"Like you're ready to be mischievous."

"What if I am?"

Avi rakes his hand over his head and moans. "I'm seriously one minute away from begging you to be mischievous with me."

"Well, now that my *safta's* okay, I want to think about you and me. And since you don't have to report back to base until tomorrow, and it's already late, maybe we can spend some alone time tonight. At a hotel."

"Really?"

"Let me weigh the options. Option 1: Go back to the base, not have a second of private time with you, get up at the crack of dawn, or Option 2: Private time alone with you. It's a no-brainer, Avi. I pick private time alone with you."

I think of Avi and me together ... all night ... in a hotel room. The word "perfection" doesn't do the fantasy justice.

"You're not still feeling super mischievous, are you?" he asks. "Because if you are, this probably *isn't* the best idea."

I can't wait to spend all night, alone, with my boyfriend. "Trust me, Avi. It's a *great* idea. Seriously, when are we going to have the chance to be alone again?"

He picks up his cell, makes a reservation at a hotel, and starts driving. Soon we arrive at a hotel on a kibbutz near Ein Gedi.

Avi pays for the room, signs papers, and gets a key from the girl at the front desk. I stand beside him, trying to act like getting a hotel room with my boyfriend is no biggie.

When in reality...

It *is* a biggie. A *real* big biggie.

Avi takes our bags and I follow him to our room. It's at the end of an adorable little one-story brick building with bright purple and yellow flowers outlining the front sidewalk. Avi opens the door and we walk inside.

When the door clicks shut, the reality of being alone with Avi hits me. I'm with my boyfriend without any parental supervision. I'm almost a senior in high school, almost an adult... in a year I'll be living on some college campus by myself, making decisions on my own.

I would never have put myself in the position of being alone with a boy in a hotel room if I didn't 100 percent trust him. I know Avi won't force me to do anything I don't want to do. The problem lies with me: I don't know if I trust myself. I admit, when I look at Avi I want him; I want him to kiss me until I can't breathe and touch me until my body melts under his touch, and I want to feel every inch of him. Will I be able to stop myself?

There are two single beds on either side of the room. They're just simple foam-filled mattresses on wooden frames that don't look very comfortable (which my parents would probably think is a good thing).

"You seem nervous," he says as he puts our bags down by the little desk. There's a chill in the air, so Avi turns off the air conditioner.

"Why do you think I'm nervous?" I look at him and remember our talk in the car about him wanting to have sex with me.

"Because you haven't said anything since we arrived."

I take a deep breath and watch intently as Avi steps closer to me. His boyish expression gives me a hint that he's just as nervous and insecure as I am.

"I'm not nervous. Really. I'm not," I say.

One side of his mouth quirks up into a smile. He doesn't believe me at all. "You want to go change in the bathroom?"

Change? As in getting in PJs?

"Sure," I say. Normally this wouldn't be a problem. This isn't the first time Avi's seen me in PJs, but this isn't just any normal ordinary night. I don't want to wear a big ol' T-shirt to bed. But I don't want to go all sexy, wearing a skimpy tank top to tease him. Okay, I admit I kinda do, so I can see how much I can affect him, but I realize that's totally selfish and manipulative.

Oh, the problems of a teenage girl are endless.

I pull out a PJ set my mom got me for the trip. It's a light blue T-shirt and matching mini-shorts. It covers enough so

I'm not showing too much cleave, but when I take my bra off in the bathroom I'm aware that the chill in the desert air is making me nippy. Over the sink there's a mirror, so I pull up my bangs to inspect George I. He's almost gone—yeah!

When I leave the bathroom, I'm holding the clothes I've worn all day clutched in front of my nippyness. Avi is sitting on one of the beds. He looks up and his breath hitches.

"You're beautiful," he says, staring at me as if I'm a goddess.

A shy smile bursts out of me. "Thanks." I look back at the bathroom. "Don't you want to, uh, wash up?"

"Yeah." But I notice he doesn't bring any PJs with him into the bathroom. I quickly toss my dirty clothes on top of my suitcase, pull out my pink satin pillow, and hop onto one of the beds. Pulling the thin sheet and blanket above my nippy parts, I wonder what Avi will sleep in. When he comes out of the bathroom, I finally know.

My mouth drops open and I swear I have to stop myself from drooling. Avi is wearing black boxer briefs. That's it. His military-ripped bod should be outlawed. He's got a serious six-pack and has muscles in places I didn't even know existed. And when my eyes wander to the bulge in his briefs, I can't help the blush that creeps into my face.

And I was worried about teasing *him*. Believe me, I'm not the teaser in this room. "You are seriously trying to tempt me, aren't you?"

He nods.

I reluctantly tear my gaze away. "Well, good night," I say, patting my pillow and pulling the covers over me. "Turn out the light before you go to sleep, will ya?"

That'll teach him to try and tease me.

But a minute after I pretend to go to sleep, I pop one eye open. He's still standing by the bathroom door looking every bit a hard-core male model with a body to die for... or at least to lose your virginity over. Knowing the guy inside the body is my one true love makes this situation almost unbearable.

"Can I at least push the beds together?" he asks sheepishly.

"I thought you were going to do it while I was in the bathroom. And then I thought since you didn't, maybe you wanted to sleep separately."

"I didn't want to push the beds together without asking you first. And then you came out here in that sexy outfit and I forgot all about it."

"It's not sexy," I tell him. "It's just a top and shorts."

"Amy, that's just about the sexiest thing I've ever seen on anyone. Maybe it's because it matches your eyes. Maybe it's because it's got lace around the edges. Or maybe it's just because you're wearing it." He looks down, embarrassed, as he pushes the beds together.

Since the frames are made of wood, there's a huge wooden gap between the mattresses. Avi folds one of the sheets into the groove and puts a blanket over it so it won't be too uncomfortable.

"What's this?" I ask, fingering the three-inch-long, olive green pouch hanging from a string around his neck.

He opens the pouch and reveals a silver metal rectangle stamped with words in Hebrew and a long number. "My ID tag. We cover it so the metal doesn't burn our skin in the heat."

There's a gold metal medallion hanging next to the ID tag. "What's that?"

He fingers the medallion. "All Sayeret Tzefa trainees get it. It has the words *Respect, Strength,* and *Honor* on it. Respect for your country, your enemies, and your comrades. Strength in body and mind. Honor to your country, your comrades, and the ones who served before you." He says it like he's had to rehearse the words for some test.

"Does everyone wear it?"

"If you're caught without it, you have to sing this stupid song to the entire squad. It's a new tradition. I think it was copied from some American Marines that did training here a few years back."

While I lie back on my pillow, Avi turns off the light.

A few seconds later I feel him sliding into bed next to me. His leg brushes mine and I hear his slow breathing. A sliver of light is shining through the window of the room, so I can make out his silhouette in the darkness. My heart is beating furiously with anticipation, especially when he turns toward me.

"Amy?"

"Yeah."

He leans on his elbow and stares down at me. "I didn't tell you this before, but I think you've been a great leader on the base."

"You're just saying that because you love me."

"I do love you. But that's not why I said it. People listen to you."

"Me? Yeah, right. It's a wonder I haven't been kicked out of the program."

"You sell yourself short. Every time your team is standing around looking for some direction, you come up with a strategy. Like suggesting taking turns with the ditch digging. And suggesting people kneel on the ground during the monkey bars on the obstacle course. Whether you believe it or not, you're a born leader."

I guess I never thought about that before. I reach up and cup his cheek. "How come you can see the good parts of me I don't even see in myself?"

"Because you're too busy focusing on negative stuff. You should stop doing that."

"I've been trying. It's kinda hard for me." I lean forward, put my hand on his bare chest, and kiss him. "I'm what you call a work in progress."

"That makes two of us." He puts his arms around me. We kiss. And kiss again. His lips are soft on mine. When he deepens the kiss and his tongue reaches for mine, the tingling sensation zings right down to my toes and back up again. I could kiss this boy forever. His kisses make me as hot as my flat iron, and I toss the covers away. My fingers trail paths around his body and his do the same. All the while, our breathing is getting faster and my pulse is racing in excitement. Our legs are intertwined, skin against skin.

I feel Avi's pulse racing too, as my palm explores his chest and abs.

Being close to Avi, his body against mine, is the best feeling in the world. It's better than eating spicy tuna sushi rolls with little pieces of crunchy tempura inside, better than drinking hot chocolate with loads of whipped cream, better than winning a tennis match.

"What are you thinking about?" he asks as I moan under his touch.

"Sushi, hot chocolate, and tennis."

"You're thinking about food? And tennis?"

He pulls away, but I take his hand in mine and weave my fingers through his. "No. I'm thinking about how being with you is *better* than sushi, hot chocolate, and tennis. What were you thinking about?"

A short laugh escapes from his mouth. "It sure wasn't hummus, falafel, and soccer."

I open my fingers so we're palm against palm. "Avi, what if we get carried away tonight?"

"We won't."

"But what if I want to? My mom bought me protection before I left, just in case. It's in one of my suitcases."

Avi takes a deep breath and leans away from me, the cool air rushing to the open space between us. I want to pull him back so his body heats mine again. Instead, I grab the covers and pull them over us. I don't know if I'm shivering from nervousness or the chilly night air.

"I'm not gonna lie to you," he says seriously. "I'm ready. Like *right now*, I'm ready."

"I think I am, too."

"Your body might be, but I know in the morning you'll regret it. And then I'll feel like crap because I knew you'd regret it." He rubs his hands over his head and moans in frustration. "You said a while back that you wanted to wait until we got married. I promised to respect that."

"I changed my mind."

"What?"

"You heard me. I changed my mind."

"Amy, you hated that you were an illegitimate child. It eats at you every day, and I think sometimes it fuels this insecurity you have. What if it happens to us? You'll never forgive yourself. Or me."

"Can you not be logical now, Avi? You're kind of ruining the mood." I sit up, thinking how right Avi is and how wrong I am. How can I let my overactive hormones rule my life? Though I must say it's kind of easy when Avi's expert fingers are strumming my body like a guitar. "Avi?"

"Yeah?"

"I'm not tired anymore. Are you?"

He shakes his head.

"We can still kiss and do other things, can't we? Remember at my house on the sofa, when my dad was working late? Can we try that again?"

Seriously, it's not like Avi and I haven't fooled around. We have. In fact, I've gone farther with Avi than with any other boy I've dated.

Avi's hands circle my waist and he guides me on top of him. My long hair shields his face as I look down at him. *"Ani ohevet o'tach,"* I tell him.

"You just said *I love you* to a girl. *Oat'cha* is for a boy."

"Ani ohevet oat'cha."

"Ani ohevet o'tach. I love you, Amy Nelson-Barak."

We kiss, and I start to move against him. My pulse is racing, and Avi's heart is pounding against my skin... and the earth is shattering into two pieces.

No, seriously.

The earth is shattering.

And we're falling.

I realize pretty quickly, through my haze of teenage sexual lust, that the earth isn't moving. Our beds are. They're moving apart and Avi and I are falling in between them. Before I know it, Avi falls to the hard cement tile floor. I'm straddling him, so lucky for me his body breaks my fall.

"Ouch," Avi says, his head banging on the tile. "I think I just got a splinter from the bed frame."

"Do you think this was a sign from God?" I ask. We *are* in the Holy Land. God can't be far away.

"More like a sign from your dad," Avi says, helping me up. "He always warns me not to touch your *parts.*"

Whether it's God or my dad or some other divine intervention, Avi and I decide it's late and we should probably get as much sleep as we can before we have to head back to the base. Instead of sleeping with our beds pushed together and having another mini-disaster, Avi sleeps on his bed and I sleep on mine.

We bridge the gap between our beds by holding hands until we both fall asleep.

24

If you don't know where you've come from,
it's hard to know where you're going.

"Have you ever been to the Western Wall?" I ask Avi in the morning when we wake up.

"Many times. I got my Bible during my army induction ceremony there."

"What's it like? Rabbi Glassman told me it's super mystical and spiritual."

Avi sits up, and I think how unfair it is that someone can look so good in the morning. Of course he doesn't have to worry about bed-head because his hair is so short.

He rubs his chin pensively.

"Well?" I say, urging him to respond.

He puts up a finger. "Yeah, um, it *is* spiritual. I'm not

orthodox, but I definitely feel closer to God when I'm there."

I narrow my eyes. "So what's all the chin-rubbing about? Don't you think I'll be spiritually moved there?"

"Definitely. But … "

"But, what?"

Avi scratches his head. "But it's got a *mechitza*. You know, a partition, separating the men from the women."

"I'm okay with that. Rabbi Glassman said it's tradition in more religious synagogues to separate men and women so they can concentrate on praying and not each other. If you're with me, I'll definitely be distracted."

"And you're okay with it even if the men's side is four times the size of the women's?"

Think positive, Amy. "Um, sure."

"And women aren't supposed to pray out loud."

"And men … "

" … pray out loud," he says, wincing in anticipation of my reaction.

Truth is, I'm okay with it. I'm going with the flow. Even if I don't observe all of the Jewish rules and traditions, I respect the people who do.

"We have time this morning, if you want me to take you there. We'll be backtracking a bit, but it's okay."

"Really?"

"Sure."

"What time does it open?"

"It's always open, Amy. Come on, let's get ready so

we can get back to the base on time. Make sure you wear something that covers your knees and shoulders. No tanks or shorts."

It doesn't take long before we're showered, dressed, and heading back toward Jerusalem.

We park a few blocks from the Western Wall. The scenery mixes the old with the new. When we come up to the Wall, the big ancient stones stacked one on top of another reach out to the sky.

I breathe in slowly as I take in the scene. There's a big area farther from the Wall where people can walk, but if you want to go closer, there's a partition.

Directly in front of the Wall, people are praying. The men bob up and down, deep in prayer, facing the Wall. Women, on the right side of the partition, pray just as fervently (albeit more quietly) on their side.

"Jerusalem was destroyed nine times," Avi explains as he covers his head with a small, round *kippah*. "But through it all, the *Kotel* survived."

Kind of like the Water Tower that survived the Great Chicago Fire, which started when Mrs. O'Leary's cow kicked over a lantern (although that historical fact has been hotly debated by the descendants of Mrs. O'Leary). Nobody debates the fact that this wall has been here for three thousand years.

"They say God is here, right?" I ask Avi. Because I'm feeling the enormity of the Wall and the attachment my Jewish ancestors have to it.

"It's the holiest of holy places for us. That's why, even when you're in America, Jews pray facing east—toward the Wall. Even in Israel, no matter where we are, we pray facing Jerusalem and the Wall. Open up and pour your heart out to God here, Amy." Avi hands me a small piece of paper and pen.

I tell Avi to go to the men's side while I head to the women's. I look up at the Wall, its chalky yellow boulders neatly stacked one on top of one another. Each boulder is as tall as my chest. The closer I get, the more I see little pieces of paper wedged in between the cracks of the stones.

Don't ask me why tears come to my eyes when I'm a few inches away from the Wall. I feel my faith getting stronger here, especially when I think about the Jews being forbidden here as recently as 1948, when Jews could only view the Wall through barbed wire. In the Six Day War, Israeli soldiers fought and died for this wall.

It makes me feel privileged just being here.

Reaching out, I touch the Wall. The ancient stones are cold, even though it's hot outside. For thousands of years, my ancestors prayed here. In the future, I hope my children come to Israel and feel this wall, considered "the gate to God."

I scribble my prayers on the paper, words to be shared only between me and God. In my head, I say the *Shema*, the holiest Jewish prayer. *Shema Yisrael! Adonai Eloheinu! Adonai Echad! Hear O Israel! The Lord is our God! The Lord is One!* and squeeze my paper inside a crack between the boulders.

I look over to the men's side and spot Avi. He's in his military uniform, touching the Wall with his hand and forehead, deep in prayer. The scene touches my heart.

God, take care of him, I pray silently. *Because he's my past, and my future.*

25

There's no shame in admitting you're an American Princess.

"How's your *safta*?" Jess asks me in the late afternoon when I join the rest of our unit in the barracks after Avi and I arrive back on base.

I organize my cubby and slide my suitcases under my bed. "She's okay. Her white blood cell counts are low, but they've stabilized her. She told me to go back and finish the program ... something about Baraks not being quitters."

"Well, I'm glad you're back."

"Me, too. By the way, Avi and I are back together."

"I knew it was just a matter of time. You guys are meant for each other."

I look at the gun resting on her lap. Guns are used as a means to help Israelis protect their land and their people.

I'm sure these guns mean something totally different to the Palestinians. "Jess, what do you think will happen between you and Tarik in the future?"

I've never asked her this before, because I know she loves him and doesn't want to think about life without him. But if it's not going to work out, why torture yourself by falling more in love with a guy you know you can't have a future with?

"I don't know," Jess says. "I don't think about it."

I think about my future all the time, and always imagine Avi in it. "Have you ever gotten in a fight and thought of breaking up?"

Jess chuckles. "Sure, but I can't stop dating Tarik any more than you can stop dating Avi. When the time comes to talk about the serious stuff, maybe we'll decide it won't work. Until then, I'm not stressing about it. Don't tell me you and Avi talk about the future."

I smile at her. "Yeah, we do."

Her mouth opens wide. "Wow. Please tell me you're not gonna get married at eighteen and skip college."

"I'm not getting married or skipping college. But I hope one day..." My voice trails off, thinking about what our life might be like in the future.

"...you'll have little Amys and Avis running around the house," Jess finishes for me.

"Maybe. But we won't name them Amy and Avi—you know most Jewish people don't name their kids after a living relative." Rabbi Glassman told me it's because of an old superstition that the Angel of Death will accidentally take the baby instead of the older relative of the same name. As if the Angel of Death would be confused. Maybe I don't believe it, but I'm not taking any chances. There won't be an Amy Jr. or Avi Jr. in my house. Naming zits is another story.

"So when did you and Avi have this discussion?"

"Last night. We stayed at a hotel in Ein Gedi."

"Just the two of you?"

"Yeah." I pull out my suitcase and pretend to rearrange my stuff.

"So? Come on, Amy. Don't keep me in suspense."

I look around to make sure nobody is eavesdropping. "We didn't have sex, if that's what you're getting at," I whisper. "I mean, I wanted to. And he wanted to."

Jess hasn't been a virgin for years, ever since she and Michael Greenberg did it sophomore year. But Jess isn't the result of two people getting together one night out of lust and nothing else; I am.

Jess waves her hand in a "come on, spill the beans" gesture. We seriously have less than five minutes before the next activity. I can't possibly describe how amazing it is that Avi and I reconnected. My body is still humming from the touch of his hands and the sound of his voice whispering sexy things in my ear, making me shiver with excitement. I'm definitely applying to colleges in Israel so we can be together whenever possible. I can't wait until our next boot camp activity just so I can see him again ... even if we can't be "with" each other. As long as we can see each other, I'm totally psyched.

Ronit comes into the barracks with Liron and they tell us to line up outside. I actually smile at Liron and don't fear that she's my rival. I pick up George II and head outside. The guys are waiting for us. I know we're going to the shooting range to practice, but I don't see anyone from Avi's unit besides Liron here.

Liron taps me on the shoulder. "Avi's not here. He wanted me to let you know that he was sorry he couldn't say goodbye."

What? Avi's not here? For how long? "Will he be back tomorrow?"

Liron shakes her head. "The Sayeret Tzefa trainees have been taken off base for intensive combat training exercises before they head to Counter Terror School. It was a surprise for everyone. Since I'm an operations specialist, I can stay on base until your unit graduates."

The thought of not seeing Avi for the rest of my trip to Israel is terrible, especially after last night. But Avi would want me to stay strong and positive.

"You okay?" Liron asks me.

Blinking back the tears about to spill out, I force a brave smile. "Yeah. I'm okay."

We're introduced to our new team leaders. There are two Israeli girls assigned as new team leaders, and three guys.

As one of the new team leaders steps in front of us, I

notice she's wearing sunglasses suspiciously similar to the $235 ones I dropped in the poop hole my first day here.

My mouth drops open. They *are* my sunglasses. I look over at Jessica, who I know also noticed because she's got the same open-mouthed, shocked expression I do.

"She fished them out," I whisper to Jess.

Jess shakes her head. "I'm speechless, Amy. What are you gonna do? Ask for them back?"

"Absolutely not!" If a girl wants those glasses so bad she'll fish in poop to get them, she can be my guest and keep them forever.

Noah got reassigned, and is also now a team leader for our unit. I wish Noah had another message from Avi, but he doesn't. I also wish I had Noah's outlook on life... no expectations, and then you won't be disappointed.

When we get to the shooting range, I walk up to Nathan as we're waiting for our turn to shoot. "Just so you know, I'm breaking up with you."

Nathan shakes his head vigorously. "Nuh uh. You can't do that. *I'm* supposed to break up with you first. That was our deal."

"So break up with me. I'm back with Avi."

"Well, you can't tell Tori. You promised to pretend to be devastated about our breakup." Nathan pouts. "How's it gonna look to Tori when she sees you broke up with me to go out with that... that beast?" He puts his arm around me and says, "Come on, Amy. You're my best friend. What's a girl best friend worth if she won't help you get laid?"

I push him away from me. "Eww. You're so gross."

"I'm a guy, I was born gross. Now go tell Tori we broke up. And that you're devastated. I want to see some tears. And don't forget to tell her I'm good in bed."

"I'm not telling her that."

"Why not?"

"Because what if it's not true? I don't want my credibility questioned."

"Are you insinuating what I think you're insinuating?"

I hold my hands up. "Don't blame me. Listen, Nathan. Ever since you broke up with Becky—"

"Bicky."

"What*ever* her name is. You don't have to act like a player. I'm only gonna say this once so you don't get a big head. You're cute, with that streaked-blond messy-haired garage-band-guy look you've got goin' on." I gesture to his hair and cute boyish face. "You're cool ... when you're not eating my white chocolate Kit Kats. And you're funny ... in an entertaining, Muppety sort of way. I'm not setting you up with Tori just so you can get into her pants. I'll set you up with Tori because you're a great guy."

"You think I'm a great guy?"

I roll my eyes. "When you're not being an idiot you are. But I've got to warn you, Tori's got issues."

"I do, too." Considering he doesn't have parents around and lives with his aunt and uncle, who aren't deliriously happy to be fostering their nephew, I'm well aware of Nathan's issues.

"There's just one more problem," I tell him, as Sergeant B-S calls us to take our places on the range.

"What?"

"Nothing I can't handle." I don't tell Nathan that while I'm trying to get Tori to fall *in* love with him, I have to get Miranda to fall *out* of love with him. Nathan may rock Miranda's world, but he doesn't feel the same way about her. That's not to say that it will never happen ... it just won't happen now. As much as I hate to admit it, Nathan and Tori have potential. They've both got *chutzpah* ... a lot of attitude and nerve. Both of them could use a person to challenge them.

"Just don't tell Tori anything that'll ruin my reputation as a stud," Nathan says as he releases the magazine to his M16.

"Don't worry, Nathan. You can do that all on your own."

The sergeant passes out bullets and tells us to load our magazines. I look down at George II. I don't have Avi to help me this time. Noah is walking behind us, making sure everyone knows what they're doing. I look over at Miranda, fitting her bullets in the magazine chamber just like everyone else. I raise my hand and wave Noah over to me.

"Hey, Amy!" he says with a big smile. "How's it goin'?"

"Good."

He kneels next to me. "Need help?"

"Not me. My friend Miranda over there ... you met her in the kitchen when we had the bee incident. She says she knows how to shoot, but that's just a cover-up. She needs help. She's just too shy to ask for it."

Noah pats me on the shoulder. "I got it. I'll go over there and *not* help her, if you know what I mean." He walks toward Miranda and kneels next to her. When she says she's okay, he stays with her and chats while she loads and aims the rifle. I think I hear her laugh at something he says right before she shoots.

I might just open my own matchmaking service when I get back to Chicago. I set up my dad and Marla this winter. Seriously, it might be hereditary ... maybe my great-great-great-grandmother was a matchmaker in some little village in Russia or Germany.

As I load George II with ammunition and get in position to shoot, I think back to my first time on the range, when Avi was lying next to me, placing my fingers into the correct position and relaxing me with his voice.

I imagine he's here with me now, acting as my support and guide. With the butt of the rifle against my shoulder, I put the rifle into the V in my left hand to steady the barrel. I settle my fingers into position, pretending Avi's hands are patiently guiding mine. As I aim at the target ahead of me and put my finger on the trigger, I take a breath and hold it while I fire.

I hit the target. Yeah!

I fire again. Another hit!

And again.

"*Avodah tovah*—nice job," I hear Sergeant B-S's voice from behind me.

I look back at his approving nod. "Thanks, sir," I say.

For the rest of the day, I remember that "nice job" and the approving nod from Sergeant B-S and it gives me strength. Until right after dinner, when Ronit gives us the news.

"Yes, the rumors are true. We're going on a night hike and sleeping in the desert tonight."

Like Noah, I force myself to have low expectations and keep a positive attitude. I can't help thinking about what *Safta* said: *You're a Barak. No Barak is a quitter.* But I also can't help thinking about desert scorpions, snakes, and hairy spiders. I'm thinking about other comforts of home as I raise my hand.

"Amy, do you have a question?"

"Yeah," I say. "Umm...is there a bathroom where we're headed?"

"Absolutely." She comes back and holds up a small shovel. "The entire place is one big bathroom. Just dig a hole and relieve yourself."

26

Being a leader sometimes means taking one for the team.

We line up with our rifles strapped to our backs and our canteens freshly filled with water. We've been told that sleeping bags will be issued at our final destination, but it might just be a rumor. What isn't a rumor is that we're sleeping in our fatigues—talk about roughing it.

The girls are freaking out about the toilet situation, so we've all come up with a plan to bring Jess's biodegradable wipies in our pockets. As a last-minute grab, I snatch my pink satin pillow off my mattress. I won't be able to sleep without it.

"What's that?" Sergeant B-S asks me in the courtyard, before we're ordered to march out. He's pointing at my pillow, which I'm clutching to my chest.

"My special pillow. I can't sleep without it."

He shakes his head. "No. *Zis* is not *beseder*—not okay. Put it back."

Well, it was worth a try. Luckily he can't see the wipies hidden in our fatigue pockets. I set my pillow back on my mattress and hurry back to Sergeant B-S and the rest of my unit.

I'm not risking another fall like I had on the night of our run, so I find myself in a slow jog next to Miranda. "Are we friends again?"

She glances at me as we jog side by side. "Yeah. I was always your friend, Amy. I just got upset for a stupid reason."

"Because Nathan was pretending to be my boyfriend? I'm sorry, Miranda. I know you like Nathan as more than a friend. It was insensitive of me to think you wouldn't care that I made a deal with him to get Avi jealous."

"It's okay. I know Nathan likes Tori. Girls like me never get a guy. Seriously, I tried to hit on Nimrod a few nights ago and he didn't even notice."

That's not a shocker, considering he's gay. "I hear he's already dating someone," I say. "What about Noah?"

"Colorado Noah?"

"Yeah," I say, feeling her out. "He's such a teddy bear, isn't he?"

"You mean chubby."

"I mean nice. Like you."

"Yeah, he's nice."

I nudge Miranda and smile. "Give up on Nathan,

Miranda. Now don't get mad at me for saying this, but I think you've been crushing on Nathan for so long because you're afraid to like someone who might actually like you back. You're stalling."

"You're acting like a therapist, Amy."

"I've been to enough of them to know what I'm talking about. Open your eyes to new people." I point to Noah, who's up ahead giving encouragement to our unit, telling us to keep going even though we're tired.

"He helped me on the range today," she tells me.

I give myself an inner high five for instigating that little moment. We jog slowly beside each other, neither of us saying anything for a while. It could be because we're panting from the jog...or it could be because my words are sinking in.

"Thanks, Amy," Miranda says eventually.

"You're welcome."

We finally get to our destination, which is a makeshift campground in the middle of the Negev desert. I can just sense the Israeli scorpions and snakes waiting for a taste of American blood. It's dark already, but the billions of stars in the sky brighten the night. I look up, wondering if Avi is looking at those same stars. I miss him so much I ache inside, but I'm trying to stay positive and strong. I've got to admit it's tough to be running and setting other people up when the love of my life, the guy who makes me want to be a better person, isn't with me.

Ronit tells us to sit in a big circle. She passes out cans of what looks like fancy dog food.

"What is this?" I ask her as I lift off the top.

"Dinner."

"Dinner?"

"It's called Loof."

Oh, no! Loof! I remember the bathroom wall with the words *Beware of the Loof!* "Don't we have pita? Or hummus?" I ask her. Listen, those are Israeli staples.

"No. It's Loof or nothing tonight. This is what the soldiers eat on missions and in desert training. Remember, this isn't a spa."

I examine the muddy brown substance. "Do you eat it with a fork or a spoon?"

"Whichever you want," Ronit tells me.

I look at my friends, all sniffing their own processed chunk of food/meat passing as a meal. I have to admit it smells like pasteurized liver, if there is such a thing. I admit I've never eaten liver before, even the chopped liver my dad made a couple of times. But it's Israel, so at least I know it's kosher and has been blessed by a rabbi.

"Plug your nose and eat the Loof," Noah suggests. "Then it's not so bad." I watch as he scoops out a chunk of the stuff and chows down.

My friends are looking at me for direction. Should we follow in Mr. Positive/No Expectations' footsteps or starve?

I could reveal that I brought my own provisions—*Kif-Kafs*—in the pockets of my pants. They've probably melted, but melted *Kif-Kafs* are probably better than Loof any day of the week.

But we're soldiers now. And Israeli soldiers eat Loof, no matter how bad it is. I plug my nose with my fingers, scoop out a chunk, and eat it. "Mmm. Yummy."

"Really?" Jess asks.

"No, not really. It's absolutely disgusting. But we're Jewish warrior women, right?"

Jess nods. Miranda nods. Even Tori nods. "Right!" they say in unison.

We look at Nathan. "Don't look at me. I'm no warrior woman. I'm not eating it."

Tori takes a tester bite from her little can. Miranda and Jess do, too. We all eat the Loof as if it's a rite of passage.

"Nathan, don't be a loser. Eat it," Tori says, tossing him a fork.

Not wanting at provoke Tori's wrath, even Nathan chows down. He's a warrior too, after all.

A truck with a pile of sleeping bags in the back is waiting for us. We're instructed to grab one and find a spot on the ground to sleep. Tori, who I haven't had a chance to talk to in a while, comes up to me.

"So how's your grandma?" she asks.

"Alive. I think she's okay, at least for now." I see a bandage on her neck that wasn't there when I left the base two days ago. "What happened?" I ask, pointing to it.

"You promise you won't laugh?"

"I promise."

Tori says, "I got stung. By a worker bee."

I suppress a laugh. "I thought you said they don't sting."

"Obviously I got my facts wrong. Subject over."

Time to start a new subject. I crane my head, looking for Nathan. Ronit is handing him a small shovel. Gross—he's about to dig himself a hole to poop in. He's probably about to Poop the Loof. I shudder thinking about it. "Listen," I tell Tori. "Nathan broke up with me."

"It probably had something to do with you staring at that guy Avi all the time," she says.

"No. It had something to do with you."

She looks at me like I'm crazy. "Me?"

"Yeah. Nathan likes you. He thinks you're pretty and fun...when you're not glaring, sneering, or insulting everyone."

Tori places her sleeping bag on the ground next to mine. "Nathan isn't my type," she says.

"Why not? Sure, he's a pain in the ass most of the time. But he's funny. And smart. And cute. And, to be honest, he's the best guy friend a girl could ever ask for. He's just about perfect."

Tori looks over at Nathan, coming back with the poop shovel. "Not interested."

I wave Nathan over to us. He tries to act cool as he says, "Hey. What's up? Mind if I sleep with you guys? I mean, uh, sleep *next* to you guys."

As he lays down his sleeping bag, head-to-head with Tori's with hope in his eyes, I tell him the truth. "Tori says you're not her type."

Tori nods to Nathan, emphasizing my statement.

"Did you tell her I was good in bed?" he asks.

I. Can't. Believe. He. Said. That.

Tori's eyebrows go up. "You guys had *sex*?" she asks me, just as Jessica lays her sleeping bag alongside ours.

Oh, man. I'm the one who's gonna need the poop shovel now for the flying bullshit about to come out of my mouth. I say a silent prayer for God to forgive me for lying. "Yeah. Nathan is better than ... better than ... better than eating a black olive without the pit."

Nathan looks at me as if I'm a total mashed potato. Jess shakes her head in disbelief. I couldn't think of anything else to say. I hate olives in general, so having sex with Nathan has got to be better than eating olives, with or without the pits.

Tori gives him one of her sneers. "I think I'll take a pass," she says tartly.

"Give me a chance," Nathan responds quickly.

"Why should I?"

Nathan kneels next to her and a sincere look washes over his face. "Because for some reason I've been itching to put a smile on your face since I met you."

"Nobody can do that."

"Won't you let me try?"

I see Tori's face softening. "You can try, but I guarantee it won't work."

"Ooh, I love a challenge." Nathan slides into his sleeping bag and rests his chin on his fists, facing Tori.

"Are you gonna watch me sleep?" she asks, trying to

sound annoyed. I notice she's not sneering, which is a good sign.

"Yeah. Watching you helps me think up lyrics to my next song. After boot camp, I'll take out my guitar and sing it to you."

Tori wipes at her eyes. Obviously nobody's ever done anything like that for her. She needs Nathan, whether she believes it or not. And he needs her.

I look around for Miranda. She's usually with us, but we're all settled and she's nowhere to be seen. I finally see her in a deep conversation with someone a few yards away—Noah. He's smiling at her. And laughing.

I slide into my own sleeping bag (after opening it and checking for snakes and scorpions) and bring George II inside it with me. George is cold on my unshaved legs, the hard metal of the barrel reminding me where we are and why we're here. Once again I think of Avi, and what military exercises he's been pulled off base to do.

"Are you wearing your bra?" Jess whispers.

"Yeah. Aren't you?"

"The wire was poking into my side, so I took it off and shoved it to the bottom of the sleeping bag. Remind me to reach down and get it in the morning."

My bra isn't at all comfortable to sleep in, but I'm keeping it on. I put a sports bra on before we left, which I'm perfectly aware makes me look like I have a monoboob shelf in front of me. But it does the job of smashing my boobs down and together so they're not bobbing up and down like a buoy in Lake Michigan when we run. Bouncing boobs is not an option.

Of course, squished boobs are not the most comfortable way to sleep. But whatever. I'm smelly from not showering, I don't have my favorite pillow, the sweat between my squished boobs is itchy, and I've got a metal rifle named George II in the sleeping bag with me. The old Amy would whine and complain. The new and improved Amy sucks it up.

As I lie here sucking it up, trying to sleep but with my eyes wide open, I glance over at Tori. I see her hand sneak out to tentatively touch Nathan's. He weaves his fingers through hers without saying a word and they fall asleep holding hands.

Which only reminds me of last night, when Avi and I fell asleep holding hands.

Argh. I can't sleep. All I can think about as I look up at the twinkling stars above me is Avi.

"I can count every single rock under me," Jess whispers. "How do they expect us to sleep?"

Now that Jess mentions it, I can feel every rock *and* *pebble* under my own body. "Maybe if we clear out the big ones it won't be as bad," I say, reaching under my sleeping bag for the big rock sticking into my backside.

Jess whimpers as she shuffles her body around. "Ouch. Remind me never to complain about my life back in Chicago."

"And remind me to appreciate my dad more. He probably had to sleep like this all the time when he was an Israeli commando," I say. "But the stars are so cool. Why don't we see as many stars back home?"

"Probably because we live near civilization," Jess says.

We both stare up into the sky. Seriously, there must be billions of stars above us. After a minute, a streak shoots through the sky. It's there and gone before I know it, making me wonder if I've even seen it at all.

"Was that what I thought it was?" Jess asks.

"I saw it, too. I've never seen a shooting star before."

"Me, either. Should we make a wish?"

I wish ... (I can't tell you, because then it might not come true. But I bet you can guess.)

As we're whispering, I have the sudden urge to pee. "I've got to go to the bathroom. Come with me."

"No way," Jess murmurs. "I'm not risking getting bitten by a night creature. Wait until morning."

I try to settle back in my sleeping bag. But since I'm not able to sleep, and I hear people snoring (Nathan is like his own little symphony), I take George II and decide to wander away from camp to find a perfect spot to squat. I need to find a place far enough away that I can take my panties and pants off, so I don't make them grosser than they already are.

Eventually I find a large, flat rock jutting out from the ground. Thankful for the little light the billions of stars offer and for the fact I don't have to dig a hole in order to pee, I situate half of my butt on the rock and the other half, well, you get the idea.

As I relieve myself, I hear little pop-pop-pops in the distance. Like gunfire. We're in Israel, on the grounds where the military does its training operations . . . can Avi be just a few hundred yards away? In the past, gunfire would freak me out, but now it's getting to be a familiar sound. I'm getting desensitized to it. Freaky, I know.

I must look ridiculous naked, from the waist down, sitting with half my butt on a rock and the other half hanging off—with an M16 strapped to my back while I'm intently listening to gunfire. If Avi could see me now (not that I'd let him see me pee, *ever*), he'd be proud that I'm roughing it without complaining.

If the Sayeret Tzefa trainees are on some sort of outdoor firing range doing night exercises, maybe I can say a quick goodbye to him. I'm aware it might not be the best idea, but I'm thinking positively. As I put my pants back on, I take a few steps toward the popping sounds.

When I hear more popping sounds, I hurry closer. Live ammo this close to the army base means training exercises, not war.

I've been walking for over ten minutes, praying that a snake or desert creature doesn't think I'm their midnight snack. I wish I had my headlight with me so I could see better. Despite the stars, the desert has too many scary shadows. I don't know if my eyes are playing tricks on me or if the rocks are really moving snakes and coyotes.

I climb up and over a steep hill. I think the firing range must be close, because the gunfire is getting louder.

As I maneuver around a big boulder blocking my path, a large, strong hand clamps over my mouth.

I try to scream as loud as I can, but the hand around my mouth tightens and my attempts at screaming are useless. I'm spun around with the force of a tornado.

27

Brilliance and stupidity are probably as closely related as love and hate.

As I'm twirled around so fast it makes my head spin, I'm face to face with an Israeli soldier. Even with his black mask and black clothes, I know it's Avi. I can see his eyes shining through the holes in his mask. I'd know those sexy eyes anywhere.

"Amy?" he whispers.

My panic starts to subside, but my pulse is still racing frantically. "Hi," I say sheepishly. "We were sleeping in the desert somewhere over there." I point in the approximate direction of our campsite. "And I heard gunfire so I thought you might be over here doing night range shooting. I know I smell because I didn't shower today. And I have sweaty cleave from my monoboob. And my underwear is full of rock dust that chafed my buttcheeks when I sat on the rock and peed. But I wanted to see you one last time before I went back to Chicago."

"First of all, *never* go toward the sound of gunfire. *Ever.* You hear me?" he says sternly.

"I hear you."

"And second—" He doesn't finish his sentence. He does curse a few times, though. Some of the words are in English, and I know some are curses in Hebrew because I've heard my dad say them on rare occasions when he's royally pissed.

I watch as Avi pushes a small button on a headset I didn't realize he was wearing. He says something in Hebrew. I can't hear the response, because the receiver must be some kind of earpiece in his ear.

"So I guess you're not doing range exercises, huh?"

He shakes his head.

"Running exercises?"

He shakes his head. "Amy, I hate to break the news to you but you've just entered military war games."

"War games? With real guns?"

"With real *paintball* guns." He picks up his rifle and shows me the gadget attached to it, which turned the gun into a paintball gun. "It's dangerous. I'm taking you back."

"I'm sorry. I just wanted to say goodbye to you. It was an innocent mistake."

"All of your mistakes are innocent, and yet they still get you in loads of trouble. Come on," he orders. He talks into his headset again as he leads me back up the mountain. He groans into the microphone, then turns to me. "I just got word from Nimrod that Ori got captured. He did manage to hide his weapon right before they got him."

"What does that mean?"

He winces, obviously pissed at this new predicament. "It means I can't take you back, not now."

"I'll go back myself, then."

"When the other team sees you walking up the mountain, it'll give away my location. I can't let you do that. It could jeopardize my team." After making me put on his vest for protection, he motions for me to follow him.

"When will this exercise be over?" I whisper.

He gives a short laugh. "When one team wins and the opposing team members are either dead or captured. Dead meaning paintball dead ... not real dead."

"Oh," I say, grateful for the elaboration.

Avi leads me over the rough terrain. I slip every once in a while because my high tops aren't exactly made for mountain climbing ... or war games, for that matter. Avi is moving quickly, holding my hand so I don't fall on my ass.

"Get down," he mouths, motioning for me to lay on the ground next to him and stay silent. "Stay here." He crawls away, and is back in less than a minute. He takes my M16 away and hands me another one. "This is Ori's. It's loaded with paintballs. They're dangerous, so don't shoot at close range and don't shoot unless fired upon."

"Don't worry." I might be a Jewish warrior woman,

but I'm not about to shoot this thing without Avi telling me to.

I move right next to him as he pulls small binoculars out of his pocket and surveys the area. He pushes that button again on the headset he's wearing and talks softly into the microphone in Hebrew.

"We'll stay here and wait for instructions from the team leader."

"Who's the team leader?"

"Nimrod."

"Why not you?"

"Because Nimrod doesn't have a civilian tagging along on the mission who also happens to be someone he's romantically involved with."

Wait. Does that mean … "Avi, were you the team leader ten minutes ago?"

"It doesn't matter."

Oh, no. It's bad enough I've been dragged into military war games because of my own curiosity and stupidity. But Avi being stripped of his team leader status because of me is awful. "Let me be captured so you can be team leader again."

He shakes his head. "Not happening."

"Why not?"

"Because this is real, Amy. Even though this isn't real war, we're supposed to act like it is. It's not capture the flag in gym class. In a real situation, I'd give my life up to protect yours. I know it and my entire squad knows it. That makes both of us liabilities."

I'm quiet as this new news sinks in. "You'd die for me, Avi?"

He pulls the mask off his face. His soul is reflected in the depths of his pupils. "I'd do just about anything for you."

Heart-melting time. I'd do anything for Avi, even die for him. I'm not sure he's convinced I'm tough enough to deal with the war games scenario. One thing I know for sure, though, is that I've single-handedly ruined my boyfriend's reputation. He got demoted because of me. How am I supposed to fix it?

Avi, oblivious to the fact that I'm ruining his military career, talks to his squad and waits. Then he talks again, getting information from Nimrod and passing back information from our end. "Doron got hit." He lets out a breath and shakes his head. "This isn't good."

"Where's Nimrod?"

"Near the other team's headquarters, where Ori is being held. Come on," he says. "Crawl on your stomach to the big rock over there. Stay low."

I follow Avi to the big rock, my knees scraping the desert floor and my monoboob pressed to the ground. I don't complain, but look on the bright side of being caught in the middle of war games: I'm with Avi.

I wished on the shooting star, and my wish came true. Next time I should specify for it not to be while he's in the middle of war games, but whatever. Being *with* Avi is better than the alternative, any day.

Avi is listening to instructions from Nimrod. He motions

me forward, so we're side by side. "Udi is covering Nimrod so he can rescue the hostage. I told them they needed a second cover man, but Nimrod ordered me to stay put."

"You think they can do it?"

"Yeah. But it's risky with us being outnumbered." Avi pulls out his binoculars and surveys the situation.

"Can you see them?"

"No. They're out of sight range."

"What happens if they're caught?"

He looks at me and shrugs. "Then it's just us."

I hear the pop-pop-pop of gunfire. Avi curses again. "Nimrod's down. Udi's captured. The other team ambushed them. Nimrod and Udi got two down before getting hit. It's just you and me," he says. "I probably don't have to tell you the odds aren't in our favor."

I'm to blame for Avi's team dying and/or being captured, one by one, as soon as I arrived. "Are you giving up?" I ask him.

"No."

"Because I have a plan."

"I do, too. It involves me opening fire when they start shooting at us. The other team knows me, and they know I'm not going down without a fight."

"I have a better plan. One that might give us the advantage."

"Let's hear it," he says, gesturing for me to share my idea.

"You'll really listen to my suggestion?"

"Of course. My girlfriend might be an American princess, and gets herself into ridiculous situations all the time ... but she's no dummy."

I straighten my back and hold my head high, ready to reveal my perfect plan. "Avi, take off your clothes."

28

---

*Who knew the best time of your life could be
on a mountain, in the middle of a desert,
caught up in war games?*

With an M16 retrofitted paintball machine gun in my hand and Avi's clothes on my body, I head into enemy territory. The mask is too big, the shirt is flimsy except in the boob area, and the pants are about to fall off, but I manage to look enough like Avi maneuvering through the rocks.

My heart is racing wildly, because I know it's just a matter of time until they realize I've got boobs and not muscular pecs. While my boyfriend is slinking around the other side in his undies, with black paint on his body (my artwork, thanks to the small container of face paint he had in his vest) and his own paintball gun, I'm the decoy.

Avi gave me specific instructions to surrender so I don't get hit. They won't fire unless fired upon. Although I know and they know that Avi would never go down without a fight.

I run from one rock to another just like Avi told me to. (Imagine one of those ducks going back and forth in a carnival shooting game.) I'm still a bit shocked he agreed to my plan, but it just goes to show that a great leader like Avi knows how to listen as well as lead. I admit it took a little coaxing from me. At first he wasn't into letting me become the target. But when I assured him I'd be okay, and that we were in this together, he finally relented.

He said to count to ten and then hold my hands over my head to surrender. But as two of the opposing team members move closer to me, cornering me on both sides, I start to panic. They're too far away to make out that it's me, but I desperately want Avi to have time to rescue the hostages from his squad and fix this botched exercise. I have to help him, even if it means opening fire to kill the enemy. I wouldn't shoot anyone in real life, because even after all of this training, I'm still totally for peace and happiness and rainbows and sushi.

But this is paintball. And I'm taking no prisoners.

I turn my gun on *auto* and shoot.

Pop! Pop! Pop! Pop!

Little paint balls are flying ferociously out of my gun. Since it's dark, I have no clue what I'm shooting, and hope I'm hitting at least some part of the enemy squad. I'm Rambo and GI Jane all wrapped into one.

Something hard whacks my back and thigh. "Ouch!" I scream. "That hurt!"

I look down at my thigh and realize I've been hit.
By a paintball.
I'm officially dead. I think.

29

Everyone should try living in the gray areas of life
at least once.

I'll have you know I took down two guys before I was paintballed to death. My idea actually worked. During the shootout, Avi was able to rescue Udi and Ori. They captured the last guy on the other team and we were victorious.

That's the good news.

The bad news (besides the paintball-sized welts I have on my thigh and stomach) is that I'm waiting in a large military tent, with Avi sitting on the chair next to me, about to be debriefed on how I got into the war games in the first place. At least they let us change back into our own clothes.

The guy who's in charge of the war games isn't Sergeant B-S. It's this other guy, with a bunch of stripes on the side of his sleeve, who happens to be sitting at a table opposite us in the tent. He's dark-skinned, bald, and does not look happy.

I don't know his rank, but he's high up there.

Considering I'm zero rank, I can't be demoted. But Avi can. And even though he personally had nothing to do with me wandering into the war games, he ended up being an accomplice.

When Sergeant B-S files into the tent, his stern eyes focus on me. This is not good. It's the same look my dad gave me when he found out I'd taken his credit card and signed him up for an online Jewish dating service.

"How did you get here?" he asks me. The bald guy with the high rank stands next to him.

I clear my throat and will myself to stay strong and positive. With Avi beside me, I get an inner strength. "I kind of wandered away from our campsite to find a place to relieve myself."

I know that telling them the entire truth—that I also wanted to say goodbye to Avi—wouldn't go over too well. I decide to play the confused American girl. I know, I know, I'm not doing my country any favors by playing dumb. But my friend Kayleigh from Georgia totally uses her southern accent to get what she wants. And this girl Renee at my school—she's super-smart and super-blond—plays the dumb blond so that guys give her attention and come to her rescue even if she doesn't need rescuing.

Who says I can't play the game for my and Avi's benefit? They don't call it war *games* for nothing.

"I got lost," I lie. "So I followed noises, hoping it would lead me back to the campsite."

Sergeant B-S huffs at my explanation and definitely looks skeptical. "Gefen," he says, staring solidly at Avi. "Why did she have a paintball gun in her possession?"

Avi quickly glances at me, then looks at the sergeant and the bald guy. "After I found her wandering on the rocks, and realized I couldn't take her back without revealing my location to the enemy when we were already down by two men, I recruited her."

"*Recruited* her? Instead of *protected* her? She's a civilian. That was bad judgment, Gefen," the bald guy pipes in. "What right did you have to *recruit* her?"

"I was team leader. I made the decision based on my professional opinion of her abilities."

The bald guy crosses his arms over his chest. "You've got to be kidding me."

I raise my hand tentatively.

"What?" he barks at me, just as the rest of Avi's squad enters the tent.

"Sir, I might not be Israeli, but my father is. He was a commando. And my boyfriend is a Sayeret Tzefa trainee. I'm trained in Krav Maga and I've just spent time in boot camp."

"She's a good soldier," Nimrod says from behind Sergeant B-S. "If it weren't for her being a decoy, our squad would have lost. Avi made the right decision."

"*Ze nachon*—it's true," Ori says.

Nimrod shrugs. "It was quick thinking on Avi's part. And Amy's, too. Protecting someone unarmed would have put him at a further disadvantage, so he gave her the means to protect herself."

Sergeant B-S turns to Avi's current superior. "Commander, what's your assessment?"

The bald commander stares at Avi and me. "I think Gefen should be reprimanded for not following procedure. And commended for his quick thinking."

"Does that mean he's not in trouble?" I ask hopefully.

"That means he gets the pleasure of running extra kilometers every day for the next week," the commander says.

"Don't think *you're* free and clear of this mess, Ms. Nelson-Barak," Sergeant B-S tells me. "I'm thinking of assigning you permanent kitchen duty until you leave."

Ugh. Not again. Picking bees out of jam, brushing ants off bread. *Amy, look on the bright side,* I tell myself. Well, at least I'm not going to be eating any more Loof. Next to Loof, the food back on base is an absolute delicacy. How's that for positivity?

"Move out, everyone," Sergeant B-S calls out. "You've got a few hours to sleep before wakeup." He then tells me that Liron is waiting for us in a military jeep to drive us back to the campsite.

I look over at Avi, and a wave of sadness washes over me. What if I don't see him for another year?

"I'll give you five minutes, Gefen." Sergeant B-S points to Nimrod. "Stay here as chaperone."

Nimrod nods, then when everyone leaves the tent besides the three of us, Nimrod turns around and gives us what little privacy he can.

Avi takes me in his arms and holds me close.

A lump forms in my throat and tears well in my eyes. I can't keep the first tear from falling. Avi holds my face in his hands and swipes the tear away.

"Tell her you love her already," Nimrod says, his back still to us.

"She already knows I do," Avi says.

"Girls like to be told."

"How would you know?" Avi shoots back.

Nimrod shrugs. "I don't. I'm guessing."

Avi leans down and kisses me, his lips warm and gentle. I pull him closer, not wanting to let him go.

When Nimrod coughs out a one-minute warning, Avi pulls back. We're both breathless. "Be good and stay out of trouble," he tells me.

"It's me you're talking to, Avi."

He smiles. "Yeah, I know. Forget what I said. Be spontaneous. It's what makes you special. I love that about you."

"I have a new motto in life. Wanna know what it is?"

"Yeah."

"Everything in the end is going to be *sababa*. You and me, my mom's new baby, my dad and Marla...even Jessica and Tarik."

"You want to know my new motto, Amy?"

"Yeah."

"Gefen, I hate to break up this *sababa* party," Nimrod says. "But time's up. Your girlfriend's got to go." He puts his hands up in mock surrender. "Sergeant's orders."

"Go," Avi whispers in my ear. "Before I'm tempted to go with you."

"Wait," I say, as Sergeant B-S bellows my name and orders me out of the tent. "What's your motto?"

Avi winks at me. "Look in your pockets when you get back tonight."

I hop in the back of the jeep Liron is driving. Sergeant B-S is sitting in the front seat next to her. I'm frantically searching for whatever Avi left for me in one of my pockets. I reach in and pull out a piece of crumpled paper. When I open it, Avi's Sayeret Tzefa medallion drops into my hand. I remember the words he said were etched on it: *Respect*, *Strength*, and *Honor*.

Back at the campground, I take my headlight under my sleeping bag and examine the medallion. The paper the medallion was wrapped in has handwritten words on it: it's a note from Avi. Tears come to my eyes as I read the words over and over...

> *You'll always hold a part of me, Amy, whether we're together or not. Love, Avi*

When I fall asleep that night, with the medallion in one hand and George II in the other, I know that even if Avi and I aren't together physically, nothing can keep us apart ever again. Well, except my dad ... especially after he finds out Avi and I stayed at a hotel alone. Dodging that bullet will prove harder than dodging those paintballs.

This adventure called my life is never dull, that's for sure!

About the Author

Simone Elkeles was born and raised in the Chicago area. She has a bachelor's degree in psychology from the University of Illinois and a master's degree in Industrial Relations from Loyola University–Chicago. She was president and CEO of her own manufacturing company before selling it in 1999 to stay home with her children. Simone started writing young adult and historical fiction novels while raising her kids and has earned numerous writing awards for her work. She strives to write emotional stories that touch the lives of her readers.

Simone loves to hear from her readers! Contact her through her website at www.simoneelkeles.com.

Don't miss the first two books about Amy and Avi:
How to Ruin a Summer Vacation
and
How to Ruin My Teenage Life